UPCHUCK
SUMMER'S
REVENGE

UPCHUCK SUMMER'S REVENGE

Joel L. Schwartz

A Yearling Book

Published by
Dell Publishing
a division of
Bantam Doubleday Dell Publishing Group, Inc.
666 Fifth Avenue
New York, New York 10103

ISBN: 0-440-40471-1

Reprinted by arrangement with Delacorte Press

Printed in the United States of America

July 1991

10 9 8 7 6 5 4 3 2 1

OPM

To MOM and DAD.
Thanks for sending me to camp.

Special thanks to Steve and Andi,
and Uncle Marshall
for their help on this book.

1

Question! What's the most horrible torture known to man and beast?

Answer! Riding in a car with my family. Impossible, you say. Listen to what happened last week.

It is a sunny Sunday and we are all in the car about to leave for the zoo. My father starts the engine and immediately turns on the most obnoxious music ever recorded. This music is so bad, it's been banned from elevators and dentists' offices.

The car hasn't even cleared the driveway when my eight-year-old sister Sally whines,

"Are we there yet?" *How can we be there,* I say to myself, *if we haven't even gotten out of the driveway?* I know I'll get yelled at if I say that out loud, so I just say, *That's number one,* to myself and pretend I didn't hear her.

"Do we have to have the radio on?" asks my mother.

"It helps me concentrate," replies my father.

"How come you won't let me play my music when I do my homework?" I ask. "It helps me concentrate too."

"That's different," replies my mother.

"Yeah," chimes in my know-it-all eleven-year-old brother, Robbie. "That's different."

I lean over ever so slightly and slide my elbow quickly and swiftly into my brother's ribs. "How is that different, Mom?"

"Richie just hit me!" screeches my brother.

"I did not!" I reply as I fold my hands on my lap and smile. "How is it different?" I ask again.

Robbie lifts his shirt and points to his ribs. "He did too, and it still hurts!"

We've gone about two miles now and without thinking I look over at Sally. "Are we there yet?" *Right on time,* I thought. *That's number two.*

Blue veins are bulging out of my father's

neck. Iiiiiiit's strrrrrroke time. "If the three of you can't behave, I'm going to turn the car around right now and we'll all go home." That never made sense to me. We act the same way at home.

"It's all Richie's fault," claims Robbie.

"I didn't do anything," pleads Sally.

"Behave, then," repeats my mother.

"Joke time!" says my father. I call it gag time, since his jokes make me gag. "Okay, everybody. Why don't anteaters ever get sick?" Everyone shrugs their shoulders and pretends to be interested. "Because they're chock full of tiny little antibodies. Ha-ha, get it?"

"I get it," says Sally. No one else even smiles. Maybe he'll stop.

"What do you call a row of rabbits, hopping backward?" Again silence. "A receding hare line. Ha-ha. How about that one?"

I look at my brother and put my index finger halfway into my throat and pretend to throw up.

My brother's laughing so hard, he almost falls off the seat. "Stop it, Richie!"

"Stop what?" I ask as I remove my finger. I can see the entrance to the zoo in the distance.

3

en I take my kids to the zoo they'll ride in
e trunk.

"Listen, kids," says my mother, "after the zoo
we're all going out to dinner and maybe a
movie."

"What? I told Paul I'd be over his house no
later than four today."

"What's the matter, Richie?" asks my mother.
"Don't you like spending time with your family?"

"Yeah, Richie," repeats my brother, "don't
you like spending time with your family?"

"No . . . I mean, yes, but—"

"Well, after today," says my mother, "you
won't have to ride with us until after you come
home from camp."

"What do you mean?" I ask.

"I just made arrangements today for you to
ride up to camp with Chuck's family. After the
summer we'll drive the two of you home."

Chuck Collins! The name made me nauseous.
When Chuck moved here two years ago, he was
without a doubt the dopiest, dorkiest dweeb in
the seventh-grade class. When God gave out
brains Chuck thought he said trains and he replied, "No, thanks, I already have a set." He

4

wasn't really dumb, he just didn't use his head. "You did what? With who? Why didn't you ask me first?"

"Chuck is such a nice boy."

He was funny looking too. Short, squashed in body, almost no neck, and a perfectly round face topped with thick black curly hair. When he ran he looked like a bowling ball with legs. "Then you ride up with him. I'm going to walk."

"Richie, what's the matter with you? I thought you told me he changed a lot this year."

I never told her that, although come to think of it, maybe he has changed a little. Now, instead of looking like a bowling ball, he looks like a knockwurst. His awful thick black-rimmed glasses have been replaced by contacts. He can take three steps in a row without tripping. "I never said that."

"You only have to ride up to camp with him," replied my mother. "Is that so bad?"

"Wanna hear another joke?" says my father.

"Are we there yet?" whines Sally.

"Richie's sitting on my side of the seat," complains Robbie.

I put my fingers into my ears and burrow my

head into the corner of the seat. Maybe my mother was right. No one would see me in the car with Chuck. I could bring along a Walkman with earphones so I wouldn't even have to talk to him if I didn't want to. Things certainly couldn't be worse than they are today. Could they?

As soon as we got home from dinner I retreated to my room and turned up the stereo full blast. No sooner had I flopped down on my bed when my mother pounded on my door. "Theresaphonecallforyou!"

"A what?"

"What?" she replied from the other side of the door.

"What?" I answered back.

"What?" she yelled.

"I can't hear you!" I replied just as she burst into the room.

Her arms were on her hips. "Turn that down!" I lowered the music so I could hardly hear it, but she continued to yell. "There's a phone call for you."

"Why are you yelling?"

Barely a centimeter from my nose her index

finger was still shaking. "I've been calling you from downstairs for over a minute. Chuck's on the phone for you."

"Chuck? Maybe he dialed the wrong number."

"Don't be a wise guy. Answer your call."

I sprang off my bed and bounded into my parents' room. Two feet from their bed I leapt into the air, turned myself around 180 degrees, and landed with a crash on my back directly in the center of the bed. Without looking I reached straight back and grabbed the receiver. "What's up?"

"My parents will pick you up at eight A.M. sharp on Wednesday," said Chuck.

"Okay."

"Are you excited about being a counselor-in-training this year instead of just a plain old camper? I'm excited. Are you excited?" Chuck asked.

Chuck's high-pitched voice reminded me of the awful sound chalk makes when the teacher scrapes it down the board. "It has possibilities, I guess."

"It ought to be fun teaching little kids how to

play ball and stuff and answering their questions about girls."

Chuck a coach of sports? Maybe dodgeball. Chuck an advisor about girls? He still thinks getting to first base with a girl is part of playing coed baseball. "Yep."

Chuck got quiet for a second and I could hear his breathing getting faster and louder. "I know I was sort of a pest to you last year in camp, but, uh, I, uh, just know this year is going to be better. You know, I've changed. I promise that there won't be a repeat of the . . ."

I remembered last summer well. Ellen didn't like me and then she did. My big chance came when I asked her to go to the lake social with me and she said yes. Then Chuck had to get involved and before I knew what was happening we were in the middle of the lake, Chuck's nose was bleeding, and he was yelling he was going to throw up. "Yeah, I remember the time we went out in the rowboat and you deposited two partially digested hamburgers and a Coke on my head."

"It sounds so disgusting when you put it that way," Chuck answered.

"It was disgusting . . . but sort of funny,

too, when I thought about it later . . . much later."

"I also promise," said Chuck, "not to—"

"Bite me in the head if we play soccer." My voice got louder as I ran my fingers across the small scar in the middle of my forehead.

"I didn't do that on purpose, you know." He sounded upset.

I was starting to feel sorry for Chuck. "I know you didn't. Anyway, what do ya say we just forget about last summer? I have a feeling this year at camp is going to be a great one too."

"Do you really think so?" replied Chuck, his voice brightening a bit.

"Sure."

"See you at eight, then," said Chuck. "You can sit next to me in the backseat."

"Okay, see ya." I hung up the phone. I wouldn't tell anybody this, but he sounded a little less nerdy today. But that was today. Tomorrow could be a different story and if there was one thing I didn't need this summer it was someone messing up my chances with girls. As for the ride up to camp, what could possibly happen in a car?

2

Wednesday morning I was up at seven. I stood in front of the mirror and looked myself over. Would the girls at camp like what they saw? I pulled in my stomach and flexed my muscles. Not bad. I turned around and tightened my back. Five feet six inches of solid steel. I leaned forward until my face was almost touching the glass. Should I shave? I pulled my upper lip out as far as it would go. I counted fifteen blond hairs. Would I ever need to shave? Oh, no. Was that a pimple just above my left cheek? There was another one on the bridge of my nose and a third on my chin. Did plastic surgeons make house calls? I needed an emergency pimple-ectomy. I slid my finger across each brownish-black spot and they disappeared. False alarm. It was only dirt.

"Richie's looking at himself again," announced my twerpy brother as he ran by my room.

He only wishes he could look this good, I thought as I pointed my finger at him. "You're dead," I yelled. I pretended to charge after him but stopped after a few steps. Chicken man disappeared into the safety of his room.

It was already seven-fifteen and I knew Chuck would be on time, so I took a quick shower and dressed. I was just bringing the last of my stuff downstairs when the bell rang. I opened the door and in tripped Chuck. He wore green plaid shorts and a multicolored tie-dyed shirt. He looked like a bad dream.

"Can I help you carry your stuff out to the car?" he asked.

I grabbed my duffel bag and tossed it to him. "Here, take this."

I don't think he was expecting me to throw it so hard, because it knocked him backward into the banister and he dropped it. It hit the floor with a thud and out popped my razor, shaving cream, and shaving lotion.

Chuck quickly picked up the things and forced them back into the duffel. "Sorry!" he said, looking over at me to see if I was mad.

Control yourself, Richie, I repeated over and over to myself. *This could happen to anybody.* "Do you think you can get my duffel into your car without destroying any more of my house?"

Chuck's voice was weak. "I think so," he replied as he took the duffel bag and shuffled slowly backward out the door.

I gathered the rest of my luggage and took it out to the car. Chuck opened the trunk and we put the stuff inside. There wasn't room for the duffel. "You shave already?" he asked.

If you call removing five hairs and a small piece of my upper lip shaving, then I've shaved. "Sure! Don't you?" I replied in a low voice so no one could hear.

"Wow!" Chuck pointed to his upper lip. "You wouldn't shave if you only had five hairs, would you?"

I laughed. "I wouldn't. After the first couple times it gets to be a pain anyway."

"If I have to do it in camp, will you show me how?"

Chuck will probably slit his throat if he tries it. "Sure. Anytime."

"Let's go," said Chuck as he jumped into the backseat. My parents were busy talking to Chuck's parents, so I waved and opened the back door. Suddenly my mother was at my side attacking me with hugs and kisses. Yech. I tried to block her with the duffel but she kept coming forward.

"Don't forget to write." My face flushed and I struggled to break her grip. "And don't forget a letter to your grandparents and Aunt Mary and Uncle Tom." I pulled free and took a step backward. "And Mrs. Thomas next door and—"

"Mom. I'm not going to letter-writing camp. If I write to all those people, I won't have time to do anything else."

"How long does it take to write a letter?"

If there was a hole I would have crawled in right then. "Mom. Please. The Collinses are waiting."

My sister came next and I bent over to give her a kiss. She shrugged her shoulders and twisted the tip of her left shoe back and forth in the ground. As soon as I'd planted a quick kiss on the top of her head, she let out a giggle and ran into the house.

"Are you going to kiss me too?" teased my brother.

"Me kiss you?" I replied. "Me kiss you?" I grabbed both sides of his head with my hands so he couldn't move and planted a big juicy kiss on his lips. Just then I heard a click. I looked up and saw Chuck standing by the car with a Polaroid camera in one hand and an instant picture in the other.

Robbie pushed me away and wiped his mouth with the sleeve of his hand. "Blech! Blech! Blech! You're weird! You're strange! You're craaaaaaaaaazy. Get away from me, you weirdo. I'm glad you're leaving early." As he ran past Chuck he grabbed the picture out of his hand. "I can't wait to show this to the girls you bring over the house," he yelled just as he disappeared into the house.

I looked back at Chuck, but he had already disappeared into the car. I'd deal with Robbie later.

My father came over last. He raised his hand

to shake, but I gave him a quick hug. "Have a great time," he said. "See you on visiting day."

"Thanks." I jumped into the back of the car, stared at Chuck, who was trying to hide in the corner, and leaned my head back on the seat. For once I would have a peaceful ride.

"Do you think I have a chance to go out with one of the girl CITs?" asked Chuck.

Chuck interested in girls? Is the world ready for this? "Sure," I replied. "Remember, if you take a girl out in a rowboat—"

"I know, no nosebleeds, no seasickness, and above all no—"

"UPCHUCKING!" we said in unison.

The car backed slowly down the driveway. I waved good-bye one more time and then my thoughts turned to camp.

"Mmmmm^{mmmmmmm}mmmmmm^{mmmmmmmm}mmm." A sound, if you could call it that, was coming from the front seat. "Mmmmmm^{mmmmmmmmm}mmm mmm." Chuck's mother was a hummer. "Mmm mm^{mmmmm}mmmmmmmmmmmmm." Chuck's mother was a half-note-off hummer. "Mmmmm mmm^{mmmmmmmm}mmmmmmm the shadow of mmmmmmmmmmmmmmmmmm^{mmmmmmmmmmm}mmm mmmmmmmmmmmm touching mmmmmmm lips and mmmmmmmm." Chuck's mother was a few-wrong-words, half-note-off hummer. I leaned my left ear up against the window and casually covered my right ear with my hand.

"We have to make one stop to get Oliver," said Chuck.

"Oliver?" I asked.

"My parents are watching him for the weekend."

"Who's Oliver?"

"You'll see," said Chuck. The car stopped in front of a two-story brick colonial house and Chuck got out. In a few minutes he returned. "Say hello to Oliver," said Chuck as a 130-pound Labrador jumped into the backseat and began sniffing my arm.

"Hi, Oliver," I replied. Oliver responded by placing his two front paws up on my shoulders and dragging his large, wet, slimy tongue across my entire face. No sooner had I wiped my face clean than he did it again. Annoyed, I pushed him away. "Get off, already!" This time he sat on my lap and leaned the side of his body against my chest. His tongue easily found the underside of my chin. "Get off!" I yelled again.

"I think he likes you," said Chuck.

"Mmmm^{mmmmmm}mmmmmm once again mmm
^{mmmmm}mmmmmm."

"I like him, too, but I'd like to get to know
him a little better before we get this serious."

Chuck gave a yank and with difficulty pulled
him over to his side. "If you ignore him, he'll
leave you alone."

I turned my back and watched Chuck's father
maneuver the car onto the expressway. When
he got into the outside lane he floored the gas
pedal and I was pinned backward into the seat.
As soon as the speedometer reached sixty he let
up on the gas and I felt myself ease forward. His
foot was heavy on the gas again when the gauge
dropped to fifty and I found myself rocking
back and forth as he tried to stay as close to fifty-
five as possible.

"Mmmmmmmmmmmmmm forever and ever
and ever and eeeeeehhhhverrrrrr mooore."

"This is going to be a great year," said
Chuck.

"Yeah," I replied as my reflection in the window began to look green.

"Mmmm^{mmmmmmmmmmm}mmmmmmm your lips
m^{mmm}mmm."

Only fifteen more miles, I thought as I

rocked backward. I closed my eyes tightly, hoping that this would stop my head from spinning. I felt Oliver sniff my leg a couple of times as I started to drift off to sleep. I dreamed I was swimming in a beautiful country lake when I heard Chuck say with some urgency in his voice, "Dad, I think . . ." Before he had a chance to finish his sentence I noticed an unfamiliar sensation in my right leg. It started out as a pleasant warm feeling but quickly changed to an awareness of something wet, smelly, and icky. My left eye slowly opened and I thought in the fuzz of being half awake I saw Oliver lifting his leg and heard Chuck ending his sentence with ". . . Oliver has to go!"

"Mmmm^{mmmm}mm warm feeling mmmmmm ^{mmmmm}mmmmm."

I looked up at Oliver and then over at Chuck. No matter which way I moved I couldn't keep the wetness away from my leg. "How much longer?" My loud voice showed my irritation. I saw Chuck's nose twitch as he tried unsuccessfully to force back a smile.

"Soon."

A vision appeared before me. Chuck and Oliver were tied on a spit that rotated slowly above a small pit filled with red-hot coals and mesquite-wood chips. I stood behind them with a fork in one hand and a sharp carving knife in the other. Chuck roast and rack of Oliver, my favorites.

The words KILL and MURDER flashed off and on in my mind. In the minute it took me to decide who would be my first victim, I felt the car slow down. I looked for the familiar CAMP TWIN PINES sign. It wasn't there. Nothing around the car looked familiar. Where were we? Why had we stopped? Then I heard Chuck's father say, "I think we just ran out of gas."

"Mmmmm^{mmmmmmmmm}mmmmmmmmm^{mmmmmmmmm}mmmmmm^{mmmmmmmmmm}mmmmmmmmmmmmm^{mmmmmmmmmmm}mmmmmm mmmmmmmm."

Are we there yet? Will we get there before the summer ends? I had my doubts.

3

It took Chuck's father half an hour to walk to the gas station and back to the car with some gas and another five minutes to drive back to the station and fill up. Even though we were running late, I ran into the men's room and tried to get Oliver's calling card off my pants leg. Not only didn't the soap get rid of the stain but it seemed to set it permanently on my khakis. Chuck's mother's solution was even worse. She poured a little perfume on the spot to get rid of the smell and the stain changed from solid yellow to pale yellow with turquoise spots. Now my pants leg looked like it had some rare tropical disease and I smelled like a dog had relieved himself in a perfume factory.

"He's never done that before," said Chuck. "I feel awful." It's better to feel awful, I thought, than to smell awful. I turned my back on him and glared at the scenery. If I only had a place to go to change. But since the stuff had gone through my pants, then my leg would smell and it wouldn't make any difference if I changed. Or would it?

As the car made its way up past the maintenance cabin on the bumpy dirt road that led into the camp, I had an idea. As soon as we stopped I grabbed my duffel and pulled out a pair of shorts. "Thanks for the ride up," I yelled as I headed back down in the direction we had just come.

When I got to the maintenance cabin I pushed the door to go in, but it was locked. I went behind the cabin and had my pants halfway down when I heard, "Richie?" The booming voice belonged to the six-feet-two-inch, muscular, no-nonsense camp head-counselor, Uncle Marshall. Was there enough time to change into the shorts? "Richie?" What would he think if he caught me half undressed here in the woods? I pulled up the smelly pants and was buttoning up as he turned the corner.

"Uncle Marshall!" I dropped the clean shorts on the ground behind me. "It's really g-g-g-g-great to see you."

He was dressed in white shorts and a blue T-shirt which had CAMP TWIN PINES written in yellow letters across the front. His balding head was covered by a yellow baseball cap with two blue pines embroidered on it. He looked mad. "What are you doing down here?"

"I wanted to—to say hello to . . . ah . . . the maintenance guys, but no one's here."

The serious expression remained as he leafed through some papers on his clipboard. "You know, we have a staff meeting now."

"I know, I was just on my way there."

He put his arm around me and we started toward the rec hall. I could feel his eyes looking me over as he started to smile. "You look terrific!" *What am I going to tell him when he asks me why I smell like Lassie?* "You really grew a lot this past year." *Or if he asks, What's that growing on your leg?* "I expect big things from you this year. There are two bunks of ten-year-olds and you'll be helping out in one." *In a few seconds we'll be in the rec hall and I'll be safe.* "This is going to be your best year, Richie. Just you wait and see."

"I'm counting on it," I replied as we entered the rec hall. Uncle Marshall slapped me on the back and walked to the front of the rec hall. Out of the corner of my eye I saw Fred and Jon, my best friends from last year, laughing and talking in the first row, but I retreated past them and sat down on the last seat of the last row.

"Hey, Richie," yelled Fred, "we saved a seat up here for you."

I wanted to be up there with them but I pretended not to hear.

"Hey, Richie!!!! Over here."

I turned completely around and faced the back, hoping they would get the message.

"Richie?" Fred's voice was getting louder. "Why don't you come up front and . . . Boy, do you smell awful."

I slowly turned around. "Hi, Fred." My face felt hot and I could barely look him in the eye. "Smell? What smell?"

Fred wrinkled up his nose and took a long, slow, deep breath. "If I didn't know any better I'd say you either fell in a vat of perfumed urine or you're wetting yourself again. Now, which is it?''

"I, uh . . . you see, I was in the car with Chuck and Oliver—"

Just then Uncle Marshall blew his whistle two times and jumped up on a bench. "I'd like to get started. Could everyone please move up closer so I don't have to strain my voice?"

"Come on up with us," said Fred again as he walked back to his seat. I shook my head no.

"Richie," bellowed Uncle Marshall as everyone turned around to look. All that was missing was a giant spotlight and a brass band. "There's a seat for you in the center of the second row." Reluctantly I stood up and slowly shuffled down to the empty seat. As I slid past each person I could hear "sniffing down the lane." *If this is a dream,* I said to myself, *now is the time to wake up.*

Uncle Marshall began by pointing to a very cute blond girl who was sitting on the end of the first row. "We'll start by everyone introducing themselves. Name? School? How many years at Twin Pines?"

The girl stood up slowly and in a very shaky soft voice said, "My name is Lisa. I'm a fresh-

man at Simonson High School. This is my first
year at Twin Pines and I'm a CIT."

My name is Richie, I repeated silently to myself. *I'm going to be your boyfriend this summer and
I'm not taking no for an answer.* I smiled, hoping
that she would look in my direction. She turned
and smiled back. *Look into my eyes. You are getting
drowsy. From now on you will listen to everything I
say. In your future is a tall, handsome, funny hunk,
who is very Rich. No, wait, that's his name, Richie.
When he gets up to introduce himself you will in-
stantly fall in love with him. You will long to run
your hands through his sandy brown hair. You will
love to stare into his shiny green eyes. You will love
looking at his muscular arms and long muscular
legggggg. Forget the legs. Don't look at the legs. The
legs are out. If she sees that stain on my pants she'll
ask me what happened. What will I tell her? I've got
to think of something fast.*

Nothing came to me until it was almost time
to speak. As I stood up and cleared my throat, I
turned my body so it faced Lisa. "Hi. My name
is Richie Harmon. I am in"—casually I lifted my
left leg and placed it on the bench so it blocked
my right. *Now she can't see the stain. You did it,
Richie. All right.* Out of the corner of my eye I

saw Lisa continuing to smile at me—"the ninth grade at Singer High School. This is my sixth year at this camp and I'm going to be a CIT this year." I flashed a return smile in her direction and sat down. Everything was going to be cool. I looked over at Lisa one more time. For some unknown reason she had turned partially away.

"Richie!" I looked around to see who was whispering my name. It was Jon. He pointed I think at my right leg and whispered something I couldn't hear.

I shrugged my shoulders and whispered back, "What?" Jon said something again, but it was still inaudible. "What? Louder!"

For some strange reason everyone got quiet just as Jon said, "XYZ! CHECK YOUR FLY!" A few people chuckled as I looked down at the open fly. It wasn't just open a little. It was open so wide, you could drive a trailer truck through it. How much had Lisa seen? I didn't want to know. I hunched over and zipped up my fly with one hand as I covered my face with the other. I was sure now this wasn't a dream. It was a nightmare.

As soon as the meeting was over I ran as fast as I could out of the rec hall down to the bunk.

I was standing in the middle of the bunk, trunk and duffel in hand, trying to decide what bed to pick when I heard, "XYZ! XYZ!" The chant was coming from outside. "XYZ! XYZ!" The door opened and in walked my three old bunkmates from last year. Bob had gotten much taller, Jon had gotten more muscular, and Fred had remained the same, even down to his stupid short haircut.

"I always knew I could count on you when I need help," I said sarcastically as we shook hands. "It's good to see you guys again, I think?" I threw my duffel on a bed in the middle on the left and Fred flopped down on the bed beside me.

"You certainly know how to impress the new girls," said Jon. "That girl Lisa on the end couldn't keep her eyes off of your—I mean you."

"What's with the stain and the smell?" asked Fred.

Before I had a chance to answer, the door flew open, smashing against the bunk behind it. In strutted a boy about my size and build. He had olive skin and his straight jet-black hair covered his ears.

"Is this the CITs' bunk?" We nodded. He quickly looked around and shook his head. "I thought the CITs would get a better bunk than this. At the camp I was at last year they even had a TV." He tossed his duffel in the air from the door and it landed on the other bed beside me a second before Jon was about to lay his things down. "My name's Jerry."

"I'm Richie and that's Fred, Jon, and Bob."

Jerry nodded at each of us before plopping himself down on his bed. "Did you see the girl in the front row? I can't wait to get my hands on her. Does anyone know when the first dance is?"

CRASH! BOOM! "OOOHH, NOOOO!" A trunk, duffel, and Chuck came flying through the door, all landing in a heap in the middle of the floor. "Who left their trunk outside in front of the door?" he asked from under the pile.

"Was that my trunk you tripped over?"

Chuck shrugged.

"If you broke my new trunk," shouted Jerry as he jumped up from his bed and ran outside, "I'll break you!" In a minute he returned dragging the trunk.

Chuck untangled himself and looked around for a bed to put his stuff on. He looked scared.

Jerry stepped in front of him, blocking his retreat. He broke into a loud laugh. "I was only kidding. This is an old trunk anyway. My name's Jerry."

"Chuck," he replied cautiously, forcing a brief smile.

"So when did you say the first dance was again?" asked Jerry.

"We didn't say," replied Fred coldly.

"I thought you old-timers knew everything about the camp. Never mind. I'll find out for myself later."

The bunk was uncomfortably silent as we made our beds and put our clothes away. If this was going to be my best year, it sure had a funny way of beginning.

4

Two birds having an argument outside my screen woke me up at seven the next morning. I was about to roll over and bury my head under my pillow when I noticed two knobby kneecaps beside my bed, staring me in the face. "I'm really sorry about what happened in the car yesterday." Had Chuck been standing there all night? "It'll never happen again!" he whined. "Honest."

Although I was still half asleep I had enough energy to slam my fist into the pillow and look him straight in the eye. "Last year you nearly ruined my summer," I barked.

"I didn't do it on purpose," said Chuck.

"Purpose schmerpose. You still did it."

"I didn't mean it," he whimpered.

"I was even dumb enough to think you had changed a little this past year at school."

"I did change!"

"After yesterday's car ride you could certainly fool me."

"But Richie—"

"Do me a favor. Stay away from me!"

"Give me another chance," he pleaded. "I promise this won't—"

"Stay away from me for the rest of this summer," I snapped.

Chuck's face reddened.

"Understand?"

Chuck nodded.

"Understand?"

"I guess so." he replied weakly. I turned my head away and waited for him to go. Chuck's breathing got louder but he didn't move. I was just about to turn around and yell at him again when I heard him shuffle away.

Enough of that nerd, already, I thought. *I need my beauty rest.* I was just drifting off to sleep again when the door to the bunk flew open and in stamped Uncle Marshall. "Rise and shine!" he bellowed. "I need everyone to do some cleanup work around the camp before breakfast!"

"No! Boo! Forget it! No way! I'm tired! Tomorrow!" we moaned.

"Bob and Jon," continued Uncle Marshall, "I want you to go to the waterfront and police the area. Fred, you and Chuck go to the rec hall and sweep it out. Richie and Jerry, there's a vine hanging down from the big oak tree at the entrance to the baseball field and it's blocking the jogging path. See what you can do to get rid of it."

"I wanna sleep! Later! Let the counselors do it!" we protested to no avail.

"By the time I count down to one I expect everyone to be out of bed and dressed!"

"What happens if we're not?" yelled Jerry.

Uncle Marshall glared at Jerry. "TEN . . . NINE . . . !"

We all jumped out of bed and quickly got dressed. Jerry jumped to his feet and threw on his clothes.

"THREE . . . TWO . . . Good. Breakfast is in one hour. That should give you plenty of time to finish." He eyed each of us one more time and then stamped out of the bunk.

"Why do we have to do this?" complained Jerry.

"This shouldn't take us too long," I replied as we walked up to the field.

"I didn't come up to camp to pull vines off trees," said Jerry. "I came up here to lie in the sun and tan my bod for the girls."

He probably scrapes the skin off his arms and smokes it, I thought. *How else would he get so high on himself?* "If we work together we can get this done in no time."

"I hope my hair doesn't get messed up," he said. *Keep talking like that and I'll mess it up personally.*

Two oak trees about fifty feet apart stood at the entrance to the field. Thick vines had completely covered the base of the smaller tree and some had even grown up over its lowest branches. The other tree had no signs of the ivy at all.

"That's poison ivy," I said.

"No way! I'm not getting near that stuff," said Jerry.

"Why don't you go back to the bunk and find

something to cover our arms and legs," I suggested. "I'll get some tools to cut the vines. I'll meet you back here." Without waiting for Jerry to answer I headed down to the maintenance cabin.

To my surprise Jerry was already back when I returned. Wedged under one of his arms was a pair of black rubber hip boots, a black rain slicker, and a black knit cap. Under the other were two pairs of red-stained, wrist-high painting gloves, and a pull-on rubber zombie mask from a Halloween costume.

"What's the mask for?" I asked.

"You wouldn't want to get poison ivy on your face, would you?"

I shook my head no.

"Well, then."

The face of the mask was white and it was covered with bloody cuts and scars. One blood-shot eye hung out of its socket while the other appeared swollen shut. The ears were pointy and deformed and there was an indentation where the nose was supposed to be. Even though it would look funny to wear, he was probably right. "Let's get the stuff off that branch first," I suggested, "and work our way down."

Jerry got a funny look on his face. He cleared his throat three times before he began. "Richie, can you keep a secret?"

"Sure," I replied without hesitation.

"I wouldn't want any of the other guys in the bunk to know this."

"Don't worry," I reassured him. "I won't say a word."

"I'm a little afraid of heights, so would you mind climbing up the tree and getting the ivy off the branches? When you're finished I'll get the stuff around the trunk."

"I don't mind," I said. "And don't worry. I won't tell anybody about it." I sat on the ground and pulled on the black rubber hip boots. I stood up and Jerry helped me on with the slicker. I tossed him one pair of gloves and I put on the other. Then I put on the mask and cap. "How do I look?"

"I'd put candy in your bag if you came to my house," replied Jerry as he boosted me up to the first branch. I was able to pull off a small amount of the vines with my hands, but the bulk of them had to be carefully chopped away.

"Hand me up the ax," I said.

"We have to hurry up and finish so I can go see the girls."

"Don't you think about anything else?" I asked.

"What else is there to think about?" he replied.

I made a weird face at Jerry under the mask as I continued to chop the thick vine. As each piece fell to the ground, Jerry picked it up and put it into the plastic bag.

"The bag's full already," said Jerry as he started down the hill. "I'll get a few more from the maintenance cabin."

I continued to chop away as I waited for Jerry to return. Five minutes went by and no Jerry. I stood up on the branches and looked. Where was he? Why was he taking so long to get the bags? I was about to jump down and go after him when I thought I heard voices coming from the hill behind me. The man's voice was unmistakable. The rest seemed female.

"And these are the athletic fields." The group was just visible at the top of the hill. "There are four baseball diamonds and two soccer fields"— Uncle Marshall was giving the new girl counselors and CITs a tour of the camp—"and a small football field just over there."

I spotted Lisa in the middle of the group and was about to call to her when I remembered what I was wearing. I grabbed the mask but it was stuck to my face with sweat. The group stopped directly under my branch. I froze.

It was really hot under the mask and sweat poured down my face and started itching my nose. As I reached up to scratch, the branch jiggled just enough to dislodge some bark. The bark bits floated downward in slow motion and landed right on Lisa's head.

She looked up and saw me sitting in the tree, hip boots, slicker, cap, gloves, mask, ax, and all. Her blue eyes widened. The screams that followed almost knocked me out of the tree. Lisa froze. The rest of the girls scattered.

"CALM DOWN," yelled Uncle Marshall as he ran down the hill after the girls.

I jumped down from the branch. "Lisa, listen." I tugged frantically at the mask. It still wouldn't budge. "It's only me, Richie!"

At first she smiled as if she understood, but when I took a step toward her she lowered her head like a blocking back and plowed right into me. The surprise attack knocked me over as she kept on running.

I looked around. Everyone was gone. The silence was finally broken by loud cackling laughter coming from the direction of the other tree. I didn't see anybody at first. Then I spotted Jerry sitting on a branch, doubled over with laughter. "That was the funniest thing I ever saw," he said.

I stood up and brushed myself off. "I thought you were afraid of heights."

"Did you see the way the girls scattered? I'll bet they all have nightmares." I continued to glare at Jerry as he scurried down the trunk. "That was really a SCREAM."

Very funny, I thought as I tore off all the protective clothing and threw it in a pile on the ground. This time the mask slipped easily off. Jerry continued to laugh. "Can't you take a joke?"

"Yeah, I can take a joke." I picked up the ax and buried it into the trunk of the tree. *We'll see how well you can take a joke sometime,* I thought but didn't say. Then I stomped back to the bunk.

5

"Nervous?" I asked.

Fred leaned against the back wall of the rec hall and shook his head no. "What time are the buses supposed to arrive with the campers?"

I looked at my watch. "They should be here any time now."

"It should be fun being a CIT," said Fred. "How old are the kids in your bunk supposed to be?"

"Ten," I replied. "Yours?"

"Seven."

"Seven?" I couldn't help from laughing out loud. "What can you do with seven-year-olds?"

"Not much," replied Fred. "Nature, arts and crafts, fishing, and major-league hiking. You're really lucky. At least with ten-year-olds you can play baseball and basketball."

"Not if they're spazzes, you can't."

"I thought you had to be older to be a true spaz," said Fred.

"I don't think so. A nerd is born a dweeb. At about age six he blossoms into a spaz and somewhere between his ninth and tenth birthday he trips into dorkdom. From there it's just a short stumble at age thirteen into full-fledged nerdiness."

Fred had a serious look on his face. "I believe you're right. After all, you are the expert on that subject."

"Expert?"

"Sure," said Fred. "That summer when we were both ten, you were the biggest dork in the bunk!"

"Since when does the fattest kid in the bunk—"

"I was not the fattest!" snapped Fred. "Tommy Slone was the fattest."

I forced myself to look serious. "At age ten

YOU WERE the fattest. So, Mr. Fatty, where do you get off calling me a DORK?"

"Honest, Richie," said Fred, "you were such a skinny spaz. Every time you swung a bat you almost fell over."

"You may have been able to hit the ball," I replied, "but it took you over an hour to waddle to first base. Come to think of it, you could have been first base."

"I was never that fat," shouted Fred as he squared off to spar with me.

I ducked his right and countered with an open-handed jab that brushed his nose. "Call me a dork, will you? Take this." My second jab caught Fred on the ear. He threw a punch with his left hand, but when I ducked under it he grabbed my head with both his hands and got me in a headlock. "Hey," I yelled in a muffled tone, "this is boxing, not wrestling."

"Let's see you get out of this, you spaz," he replied. Fred had one weakness and I went straight for it. "Tickling is no fair!" he shrieked as he grabbed my hands, letting my head go free. "Cut it out!"

Suddenly Jon, Jerry, Bob, and Chuck burst

into the rec hall. "The buses are here! The buses are here!" they yelled.

"Saved by the buses, Fred!" I joked. "One more minute and you'd have given up."

"No way!" he replied as we joined the others on the side. "One more minute and you'd be crying for help!"

Like a colony of ants the campers streamed into the rec hall and sat impatiently on the benches. When everyone was seated, Uncle Marshall started calling out bunk and counselor assignments. He began with the youngest campers. It seemed to take forever for him to finally reach the ten-year-olds.

The first boy he called was very tall and skinny. It looked like a strong wind could carry him away, possibly to Kansas. The next boy was very short. So short, in fact, that he was probably guaranteed a walk each time he was up at bat. The third was as round as he was tall. His face was covered with chocolate and three half-melted chocolate bars stuck out of his back pocket.

"Hey, Richie," whispered Jerry, "if Marshall puts me with those turkeys, I'm leaving."

Jerry was right. So far this group looked like

nerd city. "Please," I whispered quietly to myself as I raised my eyes to the heavens, "if you
make sure Jerry gets this group, I promise I'll
be"—I saw Chuck out of the corner of my eye
—"I promise I'll be nice to Chuck for the whole
summer and in school and forever. Honest. I
really haven't asked you for anything for a long
time. PLEASE!"

"What did you say?" asked Jerry.

"Oh, nothing," I replied with a smile.

The next three weren't much better. One had
a big frown on his face, one looked like he was
dressed for winter and had a runny nose, and
one had thick brownish-orange-rimmed glasses.
The last boy looked like the only halfway decent
kid in the bunch, but on his way out of the row
he caught his foot on the strap of his duffel bag
and fell with a crash to the floor.

I held my breath as Uncle Marshall said, "For
this group your counselor is Uncle Carl."

"That ain't my bunk," said Jerry loudly with a
smirk.

"And your CIT is . . . Richie."

"You got the nerds," sang Jerry. "You got
the nerds. Marshall probably picked you because—"

"Picked me because of what?" I replied as I raised my fist under his nose and inched closer. Jerry raised his fist too.

I was just about to plant a knuckle sandwich between his lips when Uncle Marshall bellowed, "Richie. Could you get with your group now so we can continue?"

I continued to glare at Jerry.

"Richie, please. Get with your bunk."

I pointed my index finger at him. "Just you wait. I'll see you later in the bunk."

"I'll be there," replied Jerry. His voice always sounded cocky. "Will you?"

I pointed my finger at him and nodded. *YOU ARE DEAD,* I thought. I couldn't imagine his parents being sorry when they heard the news. In fact they might thank me. Just outside the door I saw a rock lying on the ground and I kicked it so hard, it flew across the road and landed in a thick clump of bushes.

"See if anyone needs help with their things," said Carl.

It was tough to hide my anger. "Anyone need any help?" I snapped.

The short boy tugged at my arm and asked,

"Could you carry my duffel to the bunk for me?"

"Yeah!" I barked. "Let me have it!" I grabbed the boy's duffel out of his hand so abruptly, he looked like he might cry. *Way to make you campers feel at home,* I thought. *Might as well have said,* Hello, I'm your counselor Jack the Ripper. Welcome to camp.

"Wanna bite?" asked the fat boy as he shoved one of the half-melted chocolate bars into my face.

"No!" I snapped. He waddled away from me quickly, and behind me, all the way to the bunk. I felt bad for yelling at these guys. Jerry was really the one I was angry at. Besides, it wasn't their fault they were such losers.

"As soon as we get back to the bunk," said Carl, "everyone has to unpack, make their beds, and clean up the bunk. After that is free play until lunch."

"Great!" said the chocolate-covered fat boy. "Only a few more hours until lunch."

"Unpack? Clean up the bunk? Make beds?" mumbled the boy with the frown. "I hate to do that stuff. I knew camp was going to be a pain. I told my mom I didn't want to go, but she wouldn't listen. She never listens. I told her I'd have a lousy time but she didn't care. I wanna go home."

Standing in front of me were seven of the sorriest excuses for campers I had ever seen. Their real names wouldn't do them justice, so I gave them new ones. There was Skinny, Shorty, and Fats. The one with the runny nose would be Doc, the clumsy one would be the Spaz, the one with the glasses would be the Brain, and the one with the frown who complained would be Whiney. You've heard of Snow White and the Seven Dwarfs, well this was Nothing Right and the Seven Dorks.

So far everything at camp had gone wrong for me. I wanted to throw the three duffels I had in my hands high up into the air and yell at the top of my lungs, I WANNA GO HOME TOOOOOOOOOO!!!!!!! Instead I lowered my head and walked into the bunk. "ALL RIGHT, EVERYBODY, WHO NEEDS HELP UN-PACKING?"

It was no use. I was stuck. I tried to force a smile as I walked up to the magnificent seven's bunk the next day to help with cleanup. I was greeted by Whiney, who was sitting on the top step of the porch. His eyes were red and big tears ran down his cheeks.

I sat down on the step beside him. "What's the matter?"

He turned his back and continued to cry.

"Why are you crying?"

"I don't like this place and I want to go home."

I tried to think of what my father might say in

a situation like this, but everything that came to me sounded like him and not me. "What don't you like so far?"

Whiney wiped his nose with the back of his hand. "Everything."

"Everything?"

"Everything."

"You mean there's not one thing that—"

Whiney pulled his sweatshirt up over his head and clamped his hands over his ears. "I don't want to talk about it," he mumbled. I sat there a minute longer to see if he would change his mind, and when he didn't I went into the bunk.

Uncle Carl was sitting on his bed. "What's with him?" I asked, pointing outside.

"He's homesick. First time he's ever been away," said Carl.

"Do you think he'll leave?"

"Naw, once he gets used to things and sees how much fun it is here, everything will be all right." I sat down on the bed next to Carl. The remaining dorks were making their beds and doing their jobs. "Five minutes to inspection! Everybody get a move on it," yelled Carl.

"Can I read my science book this morning instead of playing football?" asked the Brain.

"My nose has been running all morning. Can I just watch today?" said Doc.

"These guys are going to play football?" I asked.

Carl took his clipboard and pointed to first period Monday. There in bold black letters it said FOOTBALL ON FIELD #2. "How are we going to teach these"—I almost slipped and said nerds—"kids how to play football when half aren't interested and half trip over their own feet?"

Carl smiled. "It's going to be an interesting summer, isn't it?" Interesting, I thought. How about disastrous?

At precisely ten o'clock the door to the cabin opened and in walked Uncle Marshall. "I want everyone standing by their beds at attention! NOW!" he bellowed. Everyone ran to his bed and stood as stiff and as still as possible. With a half stern and half mean look on his face Uncle Marshall checked each bed and cubby. Inside I was laughing because I remembered how scared he'd made me when I was that age.

"Not bad for the first time," he said. "Tomorrow I'll be in here with a white glove." He turned to us just before he left, so the campers couldn't see his expression, and smiled. *So it's all an act,* I thought as he left. *And I used to fall for it.*

"Sneakers and sweatshirts," said Carl. "Everyone up to field two for football."

"DO WE HAVE TO?" echoed everyone but the spaz.

"Everyone follow Richie up to field two," continued Carl. "I'll get the footballs and meet you up there."

"Last one up to the field is a rotten egg," I yelled as I bolted out the door. Halfway up the hill to the field I realized that there would be seven rotten eggs.

When Carl arrived we divided the group in two. I got Fats, Whiney, and the Spaz. We walked off to the side and the three formed a semicircle around me. "Let's start with passing," I said as I laid the football into the palm of my hand. "Put four fingers on the laces of the ball and wrap your thumb around the top." I pointed to a tree ten feet away and let the ball fly. It hit the trunk dead center. I retrieved the ball and handed it to Whiney. "Try it."

"I can't do it," he whimpered.

I probably shouldn't have, but I raised my voice. "TRY IT!"

Whiney could just about get his fingers around the ball, and as he went to throw it the ball slipped out of his hand and tumbled to the ground.

"Hold the laces tighter this time. TRY IT AGAIN." This time the ball sailed out of his hand like a wounded duck, finally dying six feet from the tree.

This was a lost cause. "I told you I couldn't do it," said Whiney as he gave the ball to the Spaz.

"Maybe next time," I said.

The Spaz grabbed the ball so tightly, I thought it might pop. He grunted like an elephant clearing his sinuses just before he let the ball go. It was wobbly and off target, but it did reach the tree. "Once more," I yelled. "Remember, laces tight and arm all the way back like you're pitching a hardball."

The Spaz twisted his body in half like a trap that sprung open just before he let the ball go. This time it spiraled a little, and for a split second, just before it veered off to the left, it looked like it had a chance to nick the tree.

"Pretty good," I said as I handed the ball to Fats.

"Can I try catching instead?" he asked.

"Okay," I replied. "Go ten steps down the field and buttonhook. The ball will be there when you turn around."

"Buttonhook? What's a buttonhook?"

I couldn't believe it. "Don't any of you guys know what a buttonhook is?"

Three blank expressions stared back at me.

"Do you see that white chalk mark over there in the center of the field?"

They nodded.

"Run as fast as you can to that spot and when you get there turn around and look at me. That's a buttonhook. DO IT!"

Fats lumbered down to the spot and stopped. In a jerky motion he turned around and held out his hands. I purposely threw the ball softly, but it didn't make any difference, because it hit him on the fingertips and fell to the ground.

"GREAT CATCH!" The voice sounded familiar, but I couldn't quite tell where it was coming from. "NEXT TIME TRY YOUR MOUTH!" Then I spotted Jerry with his bunk on field one. All his kids were laughing and pointing at us. "MAYBE YOUR BUNK

WOULD LIKE TO PLAY MINE SOMEDAY IN A GAME OF TWO-HAND TOUCH?"

Suddenly both bunks got quiet. "ANYTIME, ANYPLACE!" I yelled back.

"WE'LL GIVE YOU A COUPLE OF WEEKS TO GET READY, SINCE YOU'LL HAVE TO TEACH THEM TO WALK RIGHT FIRST!"

"YOU'LL NEED MORE THAN A COUPLE OF WEEKS TO GET YOUR MARSH-MALLOWS INTO SHAPE!" What was I saying? Was I crazy?

"LOSERS HAVE TO CLEAN THE WINNERS' BUNK FOR A WHOLE WEEK!" screamed Jerry.

"YOU'RE ON!" I replied. Seven angry campers were waiting for me when I returned.

"We can't beat them!" said the Spaz.

"Now we're going to have to clean their bunk for a week?" complained Fats.

"They're too good!" said Skinny.

"It'll be a slaughter!" said Shorty.

"If we get a handicap of seven touchdowns and the game is seven minutes long, it'll be theoretically impossible for them to score that many points if we hold the ball for at least two minutes," said the Brain.

"I don't care, I'll be at home," said Whiney.

"Richie," said Carl as he pulled me off to the side, "don't you think you should have asked the guys first if they wanted to play before you made that bet with Jerry?"

I felt awful. "I guess so," I replied as I stared at the ground. "Should I go back and tell Jerry the bet's off?"

"No," said Carl with a reassuring smile. "You'll just have to coach them as best as you can."

Maybe I should have asked the guys. Maybe I should have just ignored Jerry and his bunk. Then a funny thought entered my mind and I smiled. Maybe somehow, someway, we could beat them. Maybe?

7

"I want everybody to watch me in action tonight!" boasted Jerry as he pulled a bright yellow polo shirt over his head and tucked it into his pants. Waving around a bottle of cologne, he sprinkled some on the back of his neck and on his cheeks. "Mmmmm . . . no one can resist this. By the end of the evening Lisa and Jenny and Sara will be begging me to go out with them."

I was not impressed.

"Just to show you that I'm a nice guy, anyone who wants some of this exotic potion can come over here now and get some."

Exotic potion, I thought. *I'd sooner use water from a cesspool.* I was sure no one would take Jerry up on his offer, but I was wrong. Without hesitation Chuck walked over and said, "I'll take some."

"Sure," said Jerry as he held out the bottle. "Here." But as Chuck reached for the bottle Jerry pulled it away. "Let ME do it. You'll never get a girl unless you put it on in the right places." Jerry grabbed Chuck's shoulder and spun him around. "Close your eyes," said Jerry as he circled Chuck three times. A wild smile appeared on his face as he wildly dumped cologne all over Chuck's head, neck, back, and legs. "Ha-ha. Now you smell great."

I like to play jokes on people, especially Chuck, but this had gone too far. I jumped up from my bed. "Hey!"

"He wanted cologne. I gave him cologne. Do you hear him complaining?"

I looked over at Chuck, who had gone back to change his shirt and pants. So far he hadn't said a word. Then I looked back at Jerry. He was still laughing. I grabbed a blue shirt out of my cubby and stormed outside. Fred and Jon followed. "I can't take much more of that jerk.

He's asking for a knuckle sandwich and I may just make one for him."

"I know a better way to get back at him," said Fred as he took a step closer so no one inside the bunk could hear.

"How?"

"Tonight's the first dance, right?"

I nodded.

"Jerry's bragging about how he's going to get Lisa to like him. Right?"

"Yeah?"

"What if you got Lisa to like you instead?" asked Fred. "That would shut him up once and for all."

"That's a great idea. All I have to do is . . . is?"

"Talk to her," said Jon. "That's all."

Book reports in front of the class, campaign speeches in front of the school, are nothing compared to starting a conversation with a girl for the first time. What do you say? How do you begin? How do you end? How do you middle? What if she asks you a question you can't answer? What if you ask her a question she can't answer? What if she doesn't like sports? or cars?

or horror movies? or comic books? What if her only interest is in quilting?

"It's easy," said Fred, pointing to his mouth. "You move your lips and words come out here and they make sentences and the sentences become a conversation."

"Yes, but—"

"But nothing," said Jon. "Pretend that you're talking to Fred or me."

"But she isn't you or Fred!" I replied.

"I know she isn't me," said Jon. "But if you make her me in your mind, then you can talk to me while you're really talking to her."

"You? Her? Me? You? Maybe there's a better way to get back at Jerry," I said.

"What's the matter? Are you chicken?" asked Fred.

"Me, chicken? I'm not chicken." I wondered if a rooster has trouble talking to a chicken; do his friends say to him, *What's the matter? Are you human?* . . . "Who are you calling a chicken?" I asked.

Fred looked inside the bunk. "Jerry's combing his hair for the fiftieth time. He should be out any second. If you're not chicken, then let's get going now."

I slowly pulled on my shirt and the three of us walked up to the pool in silence. Maybe Fred and Jon were right. *All I have to do is open my mouth and talk. What's the worst thing that could happen? Nothing. Nothing's going to happen, so why am I SO NERVOUS?*

From the bottom of the hill I could see Lisa talking with two friends at the far end of the pool. "Go to it," said Fred.

I took a deep breath and started walking slowly down the length of the pool toward Lisa and her girlfriends. She was wearing black biking pants with a red stripe up the side and a white tank top. WOOOOOOW! AMAAAAZ-ZING! INCREDIBLE! BINGO! As I got closer I could feel my tongue beginning to melt and my vocal cords dissolving. When I got to where they were standing, Lisa turned toward me and smiled. Red, black, and white had become my favorite colors. I smiled back. Was I staring? Lisa smiled again and this time I waved. She waved back and I smiled.

"Hi," she said. That's when I felt my brain shut down and I lost my ability to communicate in English. I waved once more, lowered my head, and left.

"What happened?" asked Fred.

"What do you mean?" I asked.

"You didn't talk to them," said Jon.

"I couldn't!"

"You can!"

"I can't!"

"You could!"

"Jerry's on his way down the hill now," said Fred, "so it's now or never."

"Never!"

"Now!"

"Never!"

"So Richie's a chicken after all. Here chick, chick, chick," joked Jon.

"Now," I replied. I took a long, slow, deep breath and headed back toward Lisa. "You can do it. It's easy. No sweat. You can do it." I could hear the girls giggling as I approached. "You can do it! It's easy. No sweat." I was almost there. Lisa turned and smiled. "You can do it." The girl next to her turned and smiled. "It's easy. No sweat." Four more girls turned and stared. "There's no way you can do it! It's impossible! There's a lot of sweat. My sweat is sweating." This time I think I ran by them.

"You're a lost cause," said Jon.

"I can't talk on an empty stomach," I replied. "Maybe after ten or twenty hamburgers I'll be able to do it."

"One," said Fred.

"Okay," I replied.

"No excuses after that," said Jon.

"There won't be," I said.

The three of us followed our noses to the large brick grill that was just off the side of the pool. Uncle Marshall stood in front of it cooking hamburgers and hot dogs. "What'll it be, guys?"

Before we had a chance to answer, Jerry pushed in front of us. In his hand were two paper plates. "I'll take two hamburgers," he said. As soon as Jerry got his food, he pushed his way back between Fred and me and headed down the side of the pool toward Lisa.

"I thought we were here first," mumbled Jon under his breath.

"We were," answered Fred.

"What's he doing now?" asked Jon.

"He just gave one hamburger to Lisa," I said. "She's biting into the hamburger. She's chewing and smiling. Jerry's chewing and smiling. I'm not chewing or smiling. I'm sunk!"

"Maybe not," said Fred, handing me the squeeze container of catsup. "A dry hamburger tastes awful. Hurry. It's your only chance."

I looked at the red plastic container and then at my friends. Lisa and Jerry looked like they were having a good time. Was I already too late? The fate of my summer rested on the catsup.

I walked briskly down to where they were standing. "Want some catsup?" I asked. My tone was forceful and confident. Suddenly there was silence. "They have the best catsup up here at camp. It's made from tomatoes." More silence. "Fresh, juicy, giant country tomatoes."

"No, thanks," said Jerry.

Lisa picked up the top of her hamburger roll. "I'll have some," she said.

With the savoir faire of the finest French maître d' I squeezed the container. Nothing came out. I shook the container and squeezed again. Still nothing. This time I squeezed with both hands. The part of the plastic container above my hands bulged just before the top shot off. Most of the thick rich catsup from fresh juicy giant country tomatoes poured out of the container onto Lisa's hamburger until it completely buried it. A few stray drops managed to find their way onto her white top and black pants, where they left an impressionistic splatter design.

While I was searching desperately for something to say, Chuck walked by. He saw the catsup top on the ground and bent down to get it. As he stood up his head hit the underside of Lisa's plate, knocking it into her chest. Lisa looked down at the catsup oozing out around the sides of the plate that was now stuck to her shirt. Chuck panicked. In his haste to get away he bumped into me, knocking me toward the pool.

I grabbed onto the closest thing to me, Lisa's shirt. She let out a scream as we tumbled into the shallow end of the pool. The first thing I saw when I finally came up to the surface and cleared the water out of my eyes was Lisa standing there in that wet white tank top.

My mouth dropped open and my eyeballs nearly fell out of my head. "WOW!" It was the most uncool thing I had ever said, but it just popped out.

I watched Lisa's hand shoot out of the water and land on my cheek. The blow sent me reeling backward. I watched her slosh out of the pool and run back to her bunk.

My cheek was still stinging when I got back to the bunk, but it was my pride that hurt the most. I vowed to give up girls, white tank tops, and catsup for the rest of the summer and maybe for the rest of my life. Things would be safer that way.

The first person I saw after breakfast was Lisa. *Basketball, go play basketball,* I thought as I headed back to the bunk.

"Richie?"

Basketball, basketball, basketball. The thought continued to dribble around in my head. "Oh, hi, Lisa. I have to make up my basketball so I can go out and play bed."

"Huh?"

"What I really mean is . . . ah . . . uh . . . I'm really sorry about last night. I really didn't mean to really squirt you with catsup."

Lisa looked a little embarrassed. "I'm sorry I slapped you."

"That's okay," I replied. "It didn't hurt that much."

"The catsup didn't stain much either," she countered.

"So." I paused to grab a gulp of air. "You have a really loud scream."

Lisa grinned. "I'm sorry."

"It wasn't really that loud," I said. "It was sorta, you know, ahhh . . ."

"Yo, Lisa!" yelled Jerry. "Come over here. I want to talk to you."

She looked like she wanted to stay but instead said, "I gotta go. See you around."

"Yeah. See ya." As soon as Lisa and Jerry disappeared around the back of the mess hall I ran down to the bunk. Fred and Jon were making their beds and Chuck was reading.

"You'll never guess what happened," I said. "Lisa apologized."

"She did?" said Jon and Fred in unison.

"I was walking out of the mess hall and she ran over to me and said she was sorry she slapped me. We were having this great conversation when Jerry came along and pulled her away. He's such a jerk."

"Figures," said Fred.

"I can't stand that kid," said Jon.

I waited for Chuck to say something, too, but he continued to lie there silently and read. I think he finally knew that if he wanted to be alive at the end of the summer he'd better keep his mouth shut and stay as far away from me as possible.

"If there was just a way to do something to get Lisa to notice me more than Jerry," I said.

"I got an idea," said Fred. "Why don't you climb a tree dressed up in a zombie mask and—"

"Come on, guys, this is serious."

"I have an idea," said Jon, "but it's risky."

"I don't care how risky it is," I said. "I'll try anything to eliminate Jerry from the picture."

"Why don't you sneak into Lisa's bunk after taps?" said Jon. "She'll think that's cool."

I patted Jon on the back. "That's a great idea. I'm going tonight."

"TONIGHT?" said everybody.

I put my index finger over my lips. "Why

don't you announce it over the loudspeaker?'' I
snapped.

"I wouldn't rush into this, if I were you," said
Fred. "Take some time to plan out exactly what
you're going to do. You don't want to get
caught, do you?"

"I won't get caught. I'm definitely going tonight . . . and tomorrow Jerry will be looking
for another girl."

That night I almost fell asleep three times before it was time to go. At exactly one o'clock I
slipped out of bed. I put on jeans and a black
T-shirt and quietly climbed out of the bathroom
window. A bright full moon made it easy for me
to find my way to Lisa's cabin. About a hundred
yards from the bunk I found a small clump of
bushes to hide in. I tried to catch my breath. My
heart was racing and my head pounded. Suddenly I heard a branch snap behind me and I
froze.

"Richie," a voice whispered. "Wait for me."

I'd recognize Chuck's voice anywhere. "What
are you doing here?" I asked.

"Jerry said you wanted me to meet you
here," he replied.

How did Jerry know I was going? What was he up to? "I never told Jerry I wanted you to meet me."

"I'll go back, then," said Chuck.

Trouble, I thought. *Send him back.* But his voice sounded so down. *Send him back. He looks so sad. Send him back.* "No, you can stay," I said, "if you promise to be very quiet." Chuck jumped to his feet and began to dance around. "Get down and stop jumping around," I whispered through my teeth.

Chuck threw himself back on the ground. "Sorry," he whispered.

"Now, follow me over to the back door and keep low. Once we're inside, stay put by the door, while I find Lisa."

We made our way over to the bunk, up the back stairs, and in, without waking anybody. I took off my shoes and gave them to Chuck. "Hold these and don't move!" I whispered. I had started down the center of the bunk to look for Lisa when I heard two girls talking.

"The itching from this rash is so bad, I can't sleep," said one girl. Her voice was coming from outside on the porch.

"Didn't the lotion the doctor gave you help?" I recognized this voice as Lisa's.

"Not much. I'll probably be up all night again," said the first girl. "And you'll have to take the girls on their hike tomorrow by yourself."

"One thing that always works for me is . . ." The voices were getting louder, so I started inching my way toward the back door. I got there just as the front door opened and in walked Lisa and her co-counselor. I knew if we tried to leave now we'd get caught so I grabbed Chuck by the shirt and pulled him into the bathroom with me.

"Don't talk, don't breathe, don't move, don't do anything or we're dead," I whispered. Chuck opened his mouth to ask a question, but I quickly clamped my hand over it and shook my head no.

"Are you sure this works?" said Lisa's co-counselor. The voices sounded like they were getting louder and coming our way. "It sounds sort of crazy to me."

"In here," I said as I pulled Chuck into the shower with me and slid the curtain shut.

"They're coming into the bathroom. Back up against the wall and pray."

"When my grandmother told me to do this I thought it was crazy too," said Lisa, "but it worked."

Suddenly a hand reached in and blindly searched for the faucet. It narrowly missed my nose two times and Chuck's ear once before it turned the water on. Torrents of cold water started pouring down on our heads and in no time we were soaked and shivering. Then the curtain opened.

The counselor stepped into the shower sideways so she didn't see us at first. As she turned to reach for the soap she came face-to-face with Chuck. I braced myself for her scream but Chuck beat her to it. "SHE'S NAAAAAAAAA AAAAAAAAAAAAAAAAAAAAAKED!" he yelled as he bolted past her.

For a second I couldn't get my legs to move. Unfortunately my mouth did. "Amazing!"

"You creeps!" she cried.

I leapt out of the shower and almost knocked Lisa over on my way out of the bathroom. If looks could kill, my funeral would have been the next day. I opened my mouth to explain but

71

she hauled off and slapped me. This was getting to be a daily ritual. "You pervert!" she screamed.

By now all the girls in the cabin were up and they pelted me with their shoes as I fled out the back door. I jumped from the top step and landed in a heap on the cold, wet ground.

"Out for a midnight stroll?" It was hard to see at first, but the voice was unmistakable.

"Yes, no, I mean . . ." I could hear the girls outraged behind us. Standing over me was Uncle Marshall. Chuck was in his grasp beside him.

"I want to see the two of you in my office at seven A.M. sharp," said Uncle Marshall. "Now, get to your bunk before I—"

Neither of us waited around for the end of his sentence.

"Where did he come from?" I asked.

"He was outside, standing by the back door," said Chuck, "when I jumped out."

"I think you and I were just set up," I said as we continued to run for our bunk. "And Jerry's the one behind it."

9

Chuck's knees were shaking as he stood beside me in the center of Uncle Marshall's office. Inside, my stomach was doing flips. Uncle Marshall circled us slowly three times before he began. He sounded angrier this morning than he had last night.

"I'm calling your parents right now. Chuck, what's your home phone number?" Chuck opened his mouth to answer, but Uncle Marshall kept right on firing questions. "You say I shouldn't call! Give me one good reason why I shouldn't."

Uncle Marshall turned abruptly and pointed

his index finger at me. "What would your parents say if I told them you were caught in a girls' shower at midnight? How could I explain to the girls' parents that two boys were in their cabin late at night? What if you fell down and got hurt? Huh? Okay, who wants me to call your home first? Chuck? Richie?" Chuck looked over at me just as I was turning to look at him. "Well?" Did Uncle Marshall really think either of us would volunteer?

"I don't expect this kind of behavior from you," he continued. "You both know that by all rights I should send you home, but since you never did anything like this before, I won't do it —THIS TIME. Instead, for the next two days you're docked from evening activities and canteen. After dinner you go right to your bunk and stay there for the whole evening. Any questions?" We shook our heads no. Uncle Marshall walked behind his desk and sat down. "From now on I'll be watching your every movement. If I ever catch you in a girls' bunk again, you'll be on your way home in thirty seconds. Now get out of here."

Chuck and I nearly got stuck in the doorway trying to get out of there quickly. When we were far enough away from Uncle Marshall's office Chuck said, "Did you see the look in his eyes?"

I'd once seen a vampire on TV that had that look right before he bit someone in the neck. "He has to act that way so we won't do this again," I said.

"No, it was real," replied Chuck. "He was shaking his finger so close to your nose," said Chuck, imitating how it was done, "that if he got any closer I was sure he'd slice your nose right off. His breathing even sounded weird too."

I knew exactly what he meant. It sounded like a wild animal with asthma. "What are you talking about? Funny looks? Weird breathing? You probably thought he was going to kill us."

"I did," said Chuck. "Weren't you scared?"

Scared? I was petrified. "Me scared of Uncle Marshall? Naw. Let me tell you something. If he laid a hand on me, I'd tell my father and he'd be up here in a second to lay Marshall out."

"Really?" asked Chuck.

"He took karate lessons at the Y for six months a couple summers ago," I replied as I started to walk away. "He can whip anybody."

"Where are you going?" asked Chuck.

"I feel like throwing a football around. I'll be back in time for breakfast."

"Football at seven-fifteen in the morning?" he replied.

That was an excuse. I really wanted to be alone. "I want to practice throwing," I said. When I got to the football field I climbed up to the top of the bleachers and sat down. The sun was partially hidden by the trees that separated the campus from the lake and swimming pool.

Up until now my summer had been a bust. My bunk hated me, Uncle Marshall hated me, and if things continued the way they had been going, I would have a permanent imprint of Lisa's hand on my left cheek. In fact the only one that I was still sure liked me was Oliver. Big deal. I thought of writing to my father and asking him for some suggestions on how to turn things around. He would know what to do. *That's a great idea. Hmmm.*

Dear Dad,

I need help with this girl at camp. Her name is Lisa. The first day I met her my fly was open. The second day I met her I had on a zombie mask and was carrying an ax. A week later I squirted catsup all over her and pulled her into the swimming pool. The next day I was caught in the shower in her bunk at one o'clock in the morning.

Help,
Richie

That's a great idea, Richie. Send your father a letter and tell him how dumb you are. That's really smart! I buried my head in my hands and gritted my teeth. I wouldn't even want to be my friend right now. I probably would have continued feeling sorry for myself if I wasn't interrupted by a funny moaning noise coming from under the bleachers. I thought it was a wounded animal at first, but when I looked through the benches I saw Whiney huddled in a ball, shaking and crying.

"What are you doing under there?" I asked as I climbed down to meet him.

"Running away," he mumbled between tears.

"Running away?" I wiped his face with the

bottom edge of my T-shirt. "Why would you want to do that?" I asked.

"My parents won't take me out of here, so I'm running away," he replied.

I wiped his nose with the bottom of my shirt. "You still want to leave?"

Whiney nodded.

"Why?"

Whiney shrugged.

"Give me one good reason why you should leave."

"I'm no good at anything," he whined.

"Nothing?" I asked.

"Nope," he replied.

I wiped his nose again and sat him down on the bench beside me. "I have a deal for you. If I can find one thing that you're good at, you have to give camp a chance for at least a month."

Whiney continued to whimper.

"If I can't find anything," I went on, "then I'll personally help you get home."

Whiney looked at me in disbelief. "You will?"

"I promise. Is it a deal?"

Whiney thought for a long time before he shook his head weakly yes.

"Follow me," I said as we headed for the far end of the bleachers. There I picked up a football and we walked across the field toward the big oak tree. "If I can show you how to throw the football good enough so you can hit that tree, will that be enough to convince you?"

Whiney wiped his nose with his arm. "I guess."

When we were fifteen feet from the tree, I placed the ball in his hand and closed his fingers tightly around it. I pulled his arm back until it was level with his ear and asked, "Ready?" Whiney nodded. Without saying a word I walked behind Whiney and began pushing him toward the tree. When we were a foot from the trunk I stopped. "LET IT FLY!" I yelled.

"Wait a minute," said Whiney. "Anybody can hit the tree from there. You're not playing fair."

"I'm not playing fair?" I replied. "You made up your mind to go home before you ever got off the bus. Is that playing fair?" I couldn't believe I was talking this way. It reminded me of something my father would say. Whiney stood there silently and listened. "Maybe you'd like camp better if you took the time to try things instead of complaining about them." Whiney dropped the football on the ground in front of him and crossed his arms.

Maybe I should call him a wimp or a baby. That usually worked with my brother. I crossed my arms and stared back. *Oh, well,* I thought, *the way things have been going for me, I guess I shouldn't have expected otherwise.* The silence was broken by the bugle call announcing breakfast.

I turned to go to the dining room, fully expecting Whiney to run by me in tears, but instead I heard him yell, "Richie!" I turned just as he let the football go. "Wait for me," he cried. This was the first time in two weeks I had seen him smile. "I hit it dead center," he said as he grabbed my arm. "Since I have to stay till the end of the month, will you have a football catch with me every day?"

"Sure," I replied. Now I had something to write to my father about.

10

I planned to spend the first night of my prison sentence reading comics. I had the latest issue of Spider-Man™, the Incredible Hulk, and the Super Mutant Ninja Turtles. I folded my pillow in half and tried to ignore the guys as they got ready for the evening's activity.

That's when the whistling started. Loud, noisy whistling. Loud, noisy, irritating whistling followed by louder, noisier, and more irritating singing.

> "Lisa and me,
> Me and Lisa,

Tonight at the movies it'll be dark,
Oh, yeah."

What was Jerry trying to prove? My muscles tensed.

"Lisa and me,
  Me and Lisa,
  Tonight's my night,
  Oh, yeah."

That jerk. I was so angry, I nearly ripped the comic book in half. *One more remark and you're dead.*

"Want me to bring you back something to eat?" asked Fred.

"Thanks, but no thanks," I replied, still keeping my face buried in the magazine.

"Are you sure?" persisted Fred.

The whistling started again. "Listen, Fred," I snapped, "I told you I didn't want anything!"

"Well, you don't have to bite my head off," he replied.

"Sorry." I closed the comic and turned toward Jerry. "Can you cut out that whistling?"

He had a smirk on his face. "Say please."

I jumped up and threw the comic book on the bed. "You'll be the one to say, 'PLEASE STOP!' when I start pounding your face."

"Come on," said Jerry as he motioned with his hands. "I'm ready anytime you are."

I made a fist with my right hand and walked around the bed to meet him. How should I do this? Switch his nose with his right ear? Move his jaw up to his forehead? Decisions! Decisions! I hate making decisions.

I cocked my right arm and was just about to "make my day," when Jon grabbed my wrist. "If Uncle Marshall finds out you got into a fight tonight, you're as good as gone for this year." *So what?* I thought as I struggled to break his grip.

"Richie!" yelled Fred. "Don't be a jerk!"

"See ya later," smirked Jerry.

I pulled my hand free and flopped down on my bed. My face felt hot enough to fry an egg on. I folded my arms and waited for everyone else to leave before I picked up my comic again.

"Want to play cards?" asked Chuck. I didn't bother to answer. "I'm undefeated in my last ten games of old maid."

"Can't you see I'm trying to read?" I snarled.

"How about fish?"

I peered over the top of my comic. "NOT TONIGHT!"

"Will you play cards with me tomorrow night?"

What is it with him? "I don't know what I'll be in the mood for tomorrow," I replied in disgust.

"If you are in the mood will you play?"

With one hand I slowly and methodically crumpled the comic I was reading. Between gritted teeth I blurted out, "If you say one more word to me tonight it will be your last, understand?"

"Yes! I mean, no," he replied in a shaky voice. "I mean, I didn't say anything." Chuck shrank down in his bed. I continued to stare at him until he started to read a stack of letters that were sitting on the top of his cubby. Now maybe I could get some peace and quiet.

I unmangled my magazine. In it the Hulk and Spider-Man™ were fighting an army of robots. CRASH! SMASH! POW! BAM! POW! BOOM! The action was so fast and furious, I could almost hear the Hulk marching around and breathing heavily. THUMP, THUMP.

AHHHHHH, AHHHHHHH. THUMP,
THUMP. AHHHHHHH, AHHHHHH.

"Richie?" whispered a barely audible voice.

Was the Hulk talking to me? No way. Over
the top edge of my comic I saw Chuck, pale
with fright and breathing like he had just run a
marathon. AHHHHH, AHHHHHH, he
wheezed as he rocked back and forth. THUMP,
THUMP. His lips were moving but nothing
came out. Too sorry a sight to kill. I asked,
"What do you want?"

"Can I read something to you?" he whispered. "I just got a letter . . ."

"I can hardly hear you. Talk louder."

Chuck took a deep breath and began again. "I
just got a letter from my friend Murray. He's at
Camp Rainbow."

I'd been waiting all year to hear from Murray
at Camp Rainbow, I thought. "So?" I replied
sarcastically, "Why would I want to hear a letter
from your friend Murray? Do you want to hear
a letter from my friend Paul?"

"Murray is a CIT at Camp Rainbow, and
Camp Rainbow was the camp Jerry went to last
year," replied Chuck.

My patience was wearing thin. "So?"

"So listen to this," he said.

"Hey Chucky Baby:
How's it going? It's amaaaazing here. Hot
girls! Hot weather! Hot girls!"

"Get to the point," I said impatiently
"Okay," said Chuck as he scanned the letter.
"Here. . . .

"Jerry Thornton's at your camp? No way.
What a jerk. He wouldn't dare show his
face in this camp again after what he did
last year. What a rat fink he was. Every
time we planned to raid the girl's camp
he'd tell the head counselor and we'd get
caught. It took us until the last day of
camp to figure out it was him. Boy, were
we stupid. What a phony that guy is!
Bragging about himself and trying to act
cool all the time. Even the girls fell for it
until the end. Punch him out for me, will
you? I may go out for the soccer. . . .

"I guess that's it," said Chuck.
"Let me see that," I said, jumping up from
my bed. Chuck handed me the letter. Shak-

ing my head I read the letter over silently to myself. "I knew that's the way he was all the time."

I grabbed Jerry's pillow and held it up in front of my face. "JERRY, YOU'RE HISTORY. AS SOON AS YOU STEP THROUGH THAT DOOR, I'M SENDING YOUR FACE TO MARS."

"That's not the way I would do it," said Chuck.

I started to laugh out loud, which wasn't very nice. "Excuse me," I said, trying to stifle the laugh. "That's not the way YOU would do it? Since when are you part of this?"

"Didn't I get caught last night too?"

I nodded.

"Didn't I get yelled at by Marshall the Madman?"

"You did," I replied.

"I'm here with you now, right?"

I nodded again.

"Then I'm part of it."

"Thanks, but no thanks," I replied. It was a mean thing to say, but I knew if I let Chuck help, he'd eventually find a way to mess up things. "I can take care of Jerry very well all by myself."

Chuck grabbed my hand and got down on one knee. "Please let me help," he begged. "The first time I mess things up, you can get rid of me."

He looked so harmless there in front of me. But he had looked harmless before and then messed up things. "PLEASE," he begged.

I hesitated. "Okay. If you want to be the one to beat him up, then be my guest."

"I told you before, that's not the way to do it," he replied.

"What's the matter? Are you chicken to fight him?"

"No, I'm not chicken," said Chuck. "It's just that—"

"Fight him or I'm doing this on my own!"

"What if I can come up with a better way to take care of Jerry than fighting—will you let me help you then?" pleaded Chuck.

I hesitated. "You have until tomorrow night to come up with a plan. If I like it, we'll do it and you can be part of this. If I think it stinks, then I'm on my own and Jerry has to deal with my fist. Okay?"

"Tomorrow night? That's not very much time," said Chuck.

"Take it or leave it," I said.

Chuck extended his hand. "You're on!" he said. "Now do you want to play old maid?"

11

It may sound funny, but I couldn't wait for the second night of punishment to begin. As soon as the guys left to go to evening activity, I went over to Chuck's bed and sat down. "Well? What's your plan?"

"I'll have one, but I need a couple more days," said Chuck.

"It's now or never!" I replied.

"Come on, Richie. What's the rush? We have six more weeks to do something to Jerry."

"Okay. No plan. You're out," I said.

"That's not fair," said Chuck. There was a hint of anger in his voice.

"Sorry. That was our deal." I returned to my bed and took out a piece of flowery stationery I had gotten from my mom.

Chuck walked over to my bed and stared at me for a while. "Come on, Richie," he pleaded.

I didn't answer.

"Please!"

I started to write.

"JERK!"

I looked up. "Did you call me a jerk?"

"Forget it, okay?" he replied as he kicked one of my shoes halfway across the bunk and walked back to his bed.

Out of the corner of my eye I saw him rummage through his Spider-Man™ duffel and pull out a flowery piece of stationery similar to mine. He sat down on his bed and began to write something too.

"What are you doing?" I asked.

He never looked over as he said, "None of your business."

"Hey," I said, "you were the one that agreed to the deal last night."

"I only agreed because you wouldn't have let me help otherwise," he replied.

"Fine, don't tell me what you're doing," I said. "I don't really care anyway."

There was a long pause before Chuck answered, "I'm writing a letter."

"On girls' stationery?" I asked.

"It's to my friend Myron. He's always playing jokes on me, and now it's my turn to get him back. I want him to think this letter's from a girl."

"I'm doing the same thing with Jerry," I replied. "Listen to this.

"Dear Jerry,

I have something very important to give you. Meet me behind the tennis court after lunch.

Lisa

"When Jerry goes down to meet her I'll be there instead, ready to give him a knuckle sandwich."

"You're going to get yourself into a lot of trouble if you do that," said Chuck. "Jerry will tell Uncle Marshall and you'll be history."

"You may be right," I said. "Do you still want to help?"

Chuck nodded.

"Good! You can be my alibi. If anybody asks where I was, I was with you the whole day. Right?"

"I guess so," he replied.

I looked Chuck square in the eye. "What kind of an alibi are you, anyway? I was with you all day, so how could I have done anything to Jerry, right?"

Chuck turned white. "Rrrrrright. Right! RIGHT!"

I smiled and patted him on the back. "You can help me with one more thing. Do you have any envelopes with flowers on them to put this letter in?"

"No," he replied. "But I'll have one for you before lunch tomorrow."

I gave Chuck the letter. "No need to give it to me. Just put this letter into a flowered envelope and on the table so Jerry sees it when he sits down for lunch. Okay?"

Chuck nodded. By midafternoon tomorrow, I thought, all my troubles would be over.

* * *

The next day, as usual, we congregated in front of the mess hall waiting for the rest of the campers to come up from lineup and lunch to begin. All of us, that is, except Chuck. Hopefully he was inside putting my letter on the table for Jerry.

"Look who's on her way over here," said Fred.

"Who?" I asked.

"Turn around," said Fred.

I turned around just as Lisa arrived. She looked right at me and said, "How's your face?"

"Huh?" I replied.

"From the slap," she said. A big bright smile lit up her face. "It was the second one from me in twenty-four hours."

"Another slap and I'll have your handprint permanently embedded in my cheek," I replied.

Lisa glanced quickly at my cheek.

"My cheek's really okay," I told her. "Sorry I scared you again."

"Next time take your midnight shower some other place," she replied as she waved good-bye. I watched her as she walked away. She was the best.

"I did it," said Chuck. He looked very proud. "The letter's right next to his place. He can't miss it." Chuck waved a flowered piece of paper in my face. "I never read you that letter I wrote to my friend last night. Want to hear it?"

"Sure," I replied, patting him on the back. "Forget everything bad I ever said about you in the past. You're the best."

Chuck unfolded the paper and began to chuckle. "This is so funny. I can't wait for my friend to get it.

"Dear Jerry,

I have something very important to give you. Meet me behind the tennis court. . . ."

Chuck's smile turned to panic. "If that letter's here, then I must have put the letter I wrote to my friend in—"

"In there!" I yelled. "You dodo! You idiot! Everything I told you in the past is true, only double it now! Give me that letter! I'll put it inside myself."

Chuck handed me the crumpled letter and I pushed my way through the mass of campers that were already making their way into the dining room. I raced to our table and grabbed the envelope he had placed there.

"What's that?" asked Jerry.

"It's not for you," I replied.

"Then why does it have my name on it?" he asked.

I looked at it and pretended to be surprised. "So it does. I thought it said Richie." Reluctantly I handed Jerry the letter.

By now everyone was seated at the table. Jerry opened the letter and held it up for everyone to see. "It's from Lisa."

"What does it say?" asked Fred.

"Read it out loud!" urged Jon.

Just what Jerry needs, I thought, *an invitation to brag.* I saw my two days of planning going up in smoke. As for Chuck, I'd never include him in anything ever again.

Without hesitation Jerry stood up on the end of the bench and began.

"Dearest . . ."

"OOOOOOOOOO," echoed everyone at the table except me.

"I've been wanting to tell you this for a long time but every time I see you my mind goes blank. I know you will want to know this, and when you hear it you will run and tell all your friends."

Jerry paused and puffed up his chest. "I told you she loved me, guys. I'm so irresistible, every girl that sees me can't control herself." He cleared his throat for effect and continued.

"I start to tell you and I become breathless."

"OOOOOOOOOO," echoed the guys.

"You take my breath away and leave me speechless. Now there is no turning back. I cannot keep this from you another day. Once I say it you'll know why I struggled with this so. Once you hear it, your life will be changed forever.''

Jerry paused again to look at each of us and gloat. The expression on his face made me sick. I looked over at Chuck. He had a worried expression on his face.

"Believe me when I tell you that this comes straight from my heart. I mean this more than I meant anything before."

"She loves me," shouted Jerry loud enough that the tables around us got quiet and everyone listened too. "She loves me."

"I can't keep my secret any longer. . . ."

Jerry paused and I could see his eyes scan the rest of the letter. When he got to the bottom of the page the expression on his face changed from pleasure to rage. His neck became bright red and without warning he ripped the letter into pieces and dropped them on the floor. "Somebody will pay for this," he said angrily as he stomped out of the mess hall.

"What did the rest of the letter say?" asked Fred.

I retrieved the pieces and put them together. I scanned the unread part and smiled. Without hesitation I stood up on the end of the bench and puffed my chest out. My voice almost sounded exactly like Jerry's. "Now, where was I? Oh, yes.

"Believe me when I tell you that this comes straight from my heart. I mean this more than I meant anything before. I can't keep my secret any longer. Now the whole world can know.

CONTRARY TO POPULAR BELIEF
THERE IS NO TOOTH FAIRY.

IN YOUR FACE,

PSYCHE"

Everyone roared. The laughter was so loud, it blew the pieces of the letter off the table, and this time Chuck picked them up.

"I guess Jerry wasn't hungry anymore," said Fred.

"What a great letter," I said as I looked over at Chuck. He was standing at the end of the table looking like he still expected to get yelled at. "Thanks."

"You mean you're not angry?" asked Chuck.

"Angry?" I walked over to him and put my arm around his shoulder. "Your goof was my gain," I said.

Chuck smiled. "I guess that takes care of Jerry."

"Takes care of him?" I replied. "We have only just begun to fight."

12

Later that afternoon I met my bunk up on the football field for the first real practice. A group of zombies would have looked more alive. Doc had a pained expression on his face as he massaged his temples. Shorty was rubbing his eyes and Skinny was yawning. Fats was eating two candy bars at the same time and the Brain was reading the latest issue of *Popular Nuclear Physics*. Whiney sat away from the group by himself and the Spaz was under the bleachers looking for his shoe, which had fallen off. This was the group that was waiting to be molded into a winning football team? It would be easier to help the United States and Russia reduce nuclear arms.

"Who's going to win the game against Jerry's bunk?" I yelled as I raised my fist in the air.

No one answered.

"We're going to win! Right?"

Still no one answered.

"What's the matter with you guys? Don't you have any fighting spirit?"

"It's not that," replied the Brain as he peered over the top of his magazine. "The advantage in this contest of muscle and animalistic behavior lies with Jerry's gang."

"I agree with whatever he just said," chimed in Fats with a mouthful of chocolate.

"I have a headache. Can I go back to the bunk?" said Doc.

"Are you all a bunch of wimps?" Was there any question about that? "You won't stand a chance if you talk like that." *And if you don't talk like that you probably still won't stand a chance either,* I thought.

I paced up and down in front of the bleachers, pausing to look each one of them in the eye. "I don't know if we can win, either, but I'd sure like to try. Now, who's with me?"

No one moved.

"Shall I tell Jerry we give up?"

Silence.

"I'm with you," said Whiney as he walked down the bleachers and onto the field.

"Me too," said Skinny.

"Ditto," said Shorty, Fats, and the Spaz.

"My headache feels a little better," said Doc.

"Affirmative," said the Brain.

One by one they came down from the bleachers and formed a semicircle around me. "You'll be on the line," I said, pointing to Doc, Shorty, Fats, and Skinny. "You two," I continued, pointing to the Brain and the Spaz, "you'll be in the backfield." Whiney was the only one left. "You'll be the quarterback."

"Me?" asked Whiney. He had PANIC written across his forehead in sweat.

"Let's get started. Everybody line up. Now, here's what I want you to do. Shorty, you center the ball. Skinny, you run down the middle ten steps and turn around. Fats, you run to the right five steps while, Doc, you go three steps to the left. As soon as Skinny turns around, Whiney throws him the ball." I gave Shorty the ball. "One two. Hup one hup two."

Shorty centered the ball on one bounce to Whiney, who readied his arm to pass it. Doc and Fats both ran toward the center of the field instead of going left and right. Skinny ran out five steps instead of ten, and when he turned, Whiney let the ball go with all his might. It tumbled end over end, wobbled from side to side, and seemed to die just as it got to Skinny. On its downward flight the ball hit Skinny's fingertips and ricocheted straight up into the air. On its way down this time it dribbled off the top of Shorty's head, bounced onto his shoulder, rolled down his arm, grazed his knee, and fell to the ground with a thunk.

"Again," I yelled. Unfortunately the result was exactly the same.

"Let's try a running play instead," I said. "As soon as the ball is centered, everyone on the line run to the right to block. Whiney, you hand the ball to the Spaz. Place it right in his stomach as he comes around. Ready, on two. Hup one. Hup two."

Shorty centered the ball perfectly and everyone on the line ran to the right to block and run interference. Whiney turned and placed the ball softly into the Spaz's stomach. Unfortunately, when the Spaz reached down to secure the ball, it squirted out and fell to the ground. We ran the play five more times and there were five more squirts. To remedy the situation I had Whiney hand the ball off to the Brain instead. The change resulted in ten more squirts.

This was getting to be exasperating. "Time out," I said. *I need a couple minutes to come up with a play they can run successfully,* I thought. Frankly, I didn't even know if such a play existed. I was in deep thought when Whiney tapped me on the shoulder and pointed toward the other practice field. Jerry was motoring over here at a rather fast clip.

I had not seen him since the incident at lunch. His neck and face were still bright red and he was dripping with sweat. He waited until he got right in front of me before he started waving his index finger at me and shouting, "I know you put that letter on the table back there and I'm going to get you for that!"

The guys in my bunk walked around behind me. They looked a little scared. I took a step toward Jerry and pushed his finger away. "I didn't put that letter on the table and I'm ready for anything you can dish out."

Everyone expected us to start fighting, but instead Jerry smiled and said, "So you're ready for anything? Hmmmm. Does that mean that you're ready for the football game?"

Ready? I thought. *My team will never be ready.* "Sure we're ready." I could hear the guys behind me muttering, "Oh, no." "Anytime you are."

Jerry's smile got wider. "Then let's play the game next Friday afternoon."

"Friday? You mean the Friday that's nine days away from now?"

Jerry nodded.

"I thought we had until the end of the—"

Now he looked mad again. "Look, if your bunk is too chicken to play mine, then let's call the whole thing off."

"No, I didn't say that."

"Then we're set for next Friday afternoon?" he said.

The mumbling behind me was getting louder.

"Not next Friday," said Skinny.

"No way," said the Brain.

"We need more practice!" said Fats.

"Don't do it," said Whiney.

I knew I shouldn't say yes, but I couldn't say no, either, and have Jerry call me wimp. "I guess so, I mean—"

"YES or NO?" barked Jerry.

I folded my hands and looked him straight in the eye. "YES!"

Jerry grabbed my hand and shook it. "DEAL!"

I turned to go, but Jerry grabbed me by the shoulder. "I've also been thinking about our bet," he said. "You and I ought to bet too."

I shook my head. "Naw, let's leave things the way they are."

Jerry laughed out loud. "What's the matter? Don't you think you're going to win?"

Now it was my turn to feel irritated. "Win? My team's going to kill yours."

"Then bet something!" he replied.

"Well, ah . . . okay. How about if the loser buys the winner a large special pizza?" I said.

Jerry shook his head no.

"A special pizza and a large Coke?"

Jerry shook his head again.

"Then what?"

Jerry put his arm around me again as if we

were lifelong friends. I thought of it more as a boa constrictor closing in for the kill. "The loser becomes the winner's slave for one week. So if you win I'll have to do everything you say, but if I win"—Jerry paused to laugh out loud—"if I win you'll wish you never messed with me."

"No way!" I replied. He must really have thought I was stupid.

Jerry strutted around me. "Afraid?"

"No!" I could feel my whole body get tight.

"Then why not?" he asked.

"Because!" I started to walk away.

"Because you're afraid!"

"I am not!" I yelled.

"Then do it!" he yelled back.

I looked over at the seven dweebs and then back at Jerry. There was nothing I could say.

"See you Friday, if not before," he said with a chuckle as he walked away.

I stood there and watched him go. "If I perceive this correctly," said the Brain, "you have just situated yourself and us in a very precarious position."

"Will you cut it out with those fancy words?" said Shorty.

"What he means," said Fats, "is that we're all in it up to our necks"

"Precisely," said the Brain.

And sinking fast, I thought. VERY FAST!

13

It was the fourth Thursday of the summer and the day before the big game. With two practices left the team looked as bad now as they had on their first day. I was sitting by myself on the top of the bleachers looking at some football plays on my clipboard when I sensed someone was staring at me. I looked down, and standing there on the grass was Lisa. A Twin Pines T-shirt covered the top of her bright yellow bathing suit. Boy, did she look mucho "hot." I shaded my eyes with my right hand and waved. "Hi."

"What are you doing up there all alone?" she asked.

She has the best smile, I thought. "Nothing," I replied as I looked down at my clipboard. *Is that monster pimple in the center of my forehead still there? It is. I can feel it getting bigger. My hair's messed up and I smell awful. I'm not ready for this. Please leave. No, stay. Leave. Stay. She's not leaving. I can hear her walking up the bleachers toward me. Oh, no! What an awful time to get excited.*

"What's that?" she asked as she sat down beside me.

I crossed my legs and inched slowly away. It was getting bigger. "What's *what*?" My whole body felt on fire.

Lisa pointed to my lap. "That!"

I knew that Lisa would scream and I would get slapped or maybe even punched if I answered her question. "You wouldn't be interested in that," I replied.

"You might be surprised at what I'm interested in," said Lisa. "Besides, my brothers and I talk about those all the time."

I was sure my face was crimson. "You do?"

"Every Friday at dinner," she said.

The sweat was beginning to pour down my

cheeks. "Every Friday?" I gulped. "At dinner?" *I'm never going to eat dinner at her house on Friday, that's for sure.*

"The only one that doesn't get involved in the conversation is my mother. She thinks it's boring."

I wiped my forehead with my sleeve, but it continued to drip.

"But I think football is interesting," she went on.

"Football?" I asked.

Lisa pointed to the clipboard on my lap. "Those are football plays, aren't they?"

"Oh, those." I breathed a sigh of relief. "Yeah . . . yeah, they're football plays all right. What else could they be?"

"Can I see them?" she asked.

"Sure." I tilted the clipboard slightly so that it still covered my lap. *Go down. Go away.* My body refused to listen.

"I can't see them," said Lisa as she reached for the clipboard.

Instinctively I inched away.

"Richie, what's the matter?"

"The matter?" *Go down. Go away.* "Nothing's the matter." *What am I going to do? I can't keep inching away because I'll fall off the end of the bleach-ers. Maybe I can . . . brilliant.* As I slowly slid the clipboard off my lap with my left hand and gave it to Lisa I grabbed my baseball cap with my right hand and covered my problem.

"Tomorrow's the big game, isn't it?" she asked as she began to look through the plays.

"How do you know about tomorrow?" I asked.

"Jerry told me about it last night. He invited my whole bunk to come up and watch," she said.

I jumped up. "Your whole bunk!" I shrieked as my hat flew off my lap and landed on the ground under the stands. I started to cover my-self with my hand when I realized my problem had disappeared. I sat down and crossed my legs anyway just in case it decided to return. "What else did he say?"

"Nothing," she replied. "Besides, what's the big deal?"

There was still annoyance in my tone. "There's no big deal. It's just that . . . there isn't going to be much of a game. It's going to be more like a massacre."

"Why?" she asked. "What's the matter with your team?"

"Everything," I replied.

"Everything?" she echoed.

"They can't catch and they mess up every play. Outside of that they're great," I replied.

"Do you have a pencil?" asked Lisa.

"What do you want that for?" I asked.

"Maybe I can help you out," she replied.

You help me? The thought amused me. I took a pencil out of my back pocket and handed it to her. This was really going to be good.

Lisa took a minute to look through the plays again. "Hmmm . . . but if they would . . . hmmm . . . I think that might work. Can I change something here?"

"Uh . . . what are you going to change?"

"You don't think I know what I'm doing, do you?" she asked.

"It's not that . . . it's just . . ."

Lisa looked me square in the eye and shook her head. "You're just like my oldest brother, Glenn. He doesn't trust me either."

I laughed a nervous laugh. "It's not that I don't trust you, it's . . ."

Lisa looked and sounded a little annoyed.

"Both my older brothers play football and I go with my family every Friday night or Saturday afternoon to watch them play. Every Sunday the pro games are on all afternoon. I probably know as much about football as you do. Now, can I change this play or not? If you don't like it, you can change it back."

"Do it, then," I said. *Figures, she knows all about boys' stuff from her brothers but I don't know diddly about girls' things.*

Lisa tapped the eraser of her pencil rhythmically on the edge of the clipboard. "Now, if this guy stays here and that guy runs this way, then . . . hmmmm."

Is she doing this to show off? No, That's not like her. Why, then? She penciled in a couple changes and smiled. "There. That should work perfectly now. What do you think?"

At first glance the play looked exactly the same as my running play, but on closer inspection I spotted something very weird. "If I didn't know better"—and I started to laugh because the idea was so silly—"I'd say you wanted the quarterback to purposely fumble the ball."

"I do," said Lisa confidently.

"You do?" I replied with shock. "The other team can get the ball, then!"

"Not if they think the quarterback still has it," said Lisa as she became very animated. "Look. When the center hands the quarterback the ball, he purposely lets it fall to the ground. But if he hold his hands like this"—and Lisa folded her arms to show me—"the other team will still think he has it. Naturally they'll go after him, and when they do, this man"—and she pointed to the other halfback—"picks up the ball! that is lying on the ground and runs for a touchdown. It's guaranteed to work. My brother's team used it twice last season and each time they scored."

"My guys just might be able to do this play," I said. "They already have the fumbling part down pat. Thanks a lot."

I was still studying the play when Lisa glanced at her watch. "I've got to run. I'm already late for swimming."

As she got up, I stood up with her. "Can I ask you a question before you go?"

"Sure," she replied.

"Why are you helping me? I thought you were Jerry's girlfriend." Dumb, dumb question!

Lisa looked surprised. "First of all," she replied, "I'm not anybody's girlfriend just yet. And as far as why I helped you? Well, watching a massacre is very boring. Now I have a chance of seeing a good game. See ya."

A funny thought occurred to me as I watched Lisa disappear down the hill: Has any professional football team ever had a married couple as their head coaches? Maybe she could coach offense and I could coach defense. Maybe we could—

"Do we have to practice again today?"

"My back hurts."

"When's snack?"

"We refuse to play!"

Somewhere between Lisa's departure and my daydreams my bunk had arrived. "What do you mean you're not going to play?" I asked.

The Brain was their spokesman. "We refuse to humiliate our egos and annihilate our bodies!"

"If you forfeit you'll have to clean their bunk for a whole week," I replied.

"We'll have to do that anyway," chimed in Fats. "At least this way we'll do it all in one piece."

I looked at each one square in the eye. Should I beg them? No way. Maybe logic would work. Naw, then I'd have to deal with that dumb Brain. I had no choice but to act like the Incredible Hulk and use force, intimidation, and terror. I threw my clipboard on the ground. "Everyone has to play or else!" What if they ask, *Or else what?* "I don't want to hear any more questions from anybody."

Everyone stood perfectly still.

"Let's get practicing!"

No one moved until I bent over to get my clipboard, and then they all charged onto the field. I felt pretty bad about having to do things like this, but there was no way I was going to let Jerry get the best of me. They'd probably all forgive me anyway if we won.

14

I prayed for rain on Friday. It was bright and sunny. I prayed that all the footballs would somehow disappear. Uncle Marshall came up to me after lunch and personally showed me a brand-new ball he had picked out for the game. "Jerry asked me if I would referee your game today," he said. "For such an important game you need an impartial judge." Impartial judge my eye, Jerry just wanted to look good for Uncle Marshall so he could be picked for CIT of the year.

I forced a smile. "Great."

Uncle Marshall patted me on the back. "Have your team on the field by two. Good luck."

That's exactly what I would need, luck and plenty of it. After lunch I made my final preparations for the game. I put a rabbit's foot in my pocket and tied a lucky horseshoe charm around my neck. Someone once told me if you hold your breath for one minute and recite the alphabet backward to yourself seven times you can make a wish and it'll come true. Holding my breath was easy; however, I only got through the alphabet two times, with four mistakes. I made a wish anyway.

When I got to the field, all the girl CITs were already sitting in the bleachers. I gathered my team around me. Doc was holding his stomach. Shorty, Skinny, and Whiney looked petrified. The Brain was busy punching numbers into a pocket calculator. The Spaz was sitting on the ground trying to figure out how to unknot his laces, and Fats was eating a sandwich of two milk chocolate bars with a dark chocolate bar in the center.

"Everybody ready?" I asked.

"I'm ready," said Fats, pointing to his side

and back pockets, which were bulging with chocolate bars.

"I think we have a chance to beat these guys." I made sure the tone of my voice was loud and definite. No one moved, no one breathed, no one said a word. A petrified forest would have given me a more enthusiastic response. "One of us has to win. Why not us?"

"Our chances of winning are one in ten trillion!" said the Brain.

"We're going to get creamed," said Shorty.

Uncle Marshall blew his whistle. "Let's get started!" he shouted.

I patted everyone on the shoulder. "Do the best you can. Now go get 'em." Everybody put his hands into the center of the huddle and mumbled an unconvincing "We're number one?" I had started back toward the bench when I felt a tug at my pocket. It was Whiney.

"I'm scared," he said.

"So am I," I replied. "Just remember, keep the ball level with your eye and flick your wrist when you throw it. You can do it." He looked back at me twice before he got to the center of the field. I buried my head in my hands and prayed to the ancient God of Upsets.

"Good luck." I recognized Chuck's voice.

"Thanks," I replied.

"Things could be worse," he said. "You could be in a rowboat with me."

"Either way I'd get upchucked on," I replied. "This is just going to be a little bit slower and a lot more painful."

We won the coin toss and we elected to receive. *That will probably be the only thing we'll win all day,* I thought as the kickoff flew through the air. It was a long kick that sailed through the Spaz's hands, bounced off Fats's leg, and went out of bounds on the ten-yard line.

The first quarter ended in a 0–0 tie. Midway through the second quarter, however, a short pass that should have gone for just a small gain turned into a touchdown when the Spaz ran into Shorty and they both fell down. Jerry—7, Me—zip.

On the next kickoff Doc fumbled the ball and Jerry's team recovered. Three plays later they scored again. Jerry—14, Me—zip. And that's how the half ended.

Jerry was all smiles as we passed each other on the field. "One more half to go, SLAVE!" he jeered. "I'd like my bed made directly after the game. I'll decide the rest later."

I took the guys behind the bleachers and sat them down under a tree. "We're not out of it yet." The bravado in my voice hid my concern. "We'll get them in the second half!"

"According to the Gran-Horwitz formula, with us fourteen points behind at halftime the probability of us winning is"—the Brain punched some numbers into his calculator—"one in . . . the number's so big it won't fit on my calculator."

"I've seen teams like this win games," said the Spaz.

"Where?" asked Skinny.

"In the movies. Remember what happened in—"

"That's the movies," said Shorty. "This is real."

"If I were you," said a voice from behind, "I'd have the tall, skinny kid rush the passer. They'll never be able to throw over him." There leaning against the tree was Lisa. "And don't forget the FUMBLEROOSKY."

I looked puzzled. "The FUMBLE-ROOSKY?"

"The play from the other day," she replied.

"Oh, that," I replied. "I never knew they called it that. Thanks for reminding me." Lisa smiled and went back to the bleachers.

"This ought to help too," said Chuck, putting his Spider-Man™ briefcase on the ground. He took out a pair of gloves with suction cups on them. "These are my Spider-Man™ suction gloves. He uses them to walk up walls. This should help someone catch passes."

"We can't use them, they're illegal," I said reluctantly.

Chuck put the gloves back in his case. "Then you're really in trouble," he replied. "Passes bounce off your players' hands like they're playing volleyball out there instead of—"

"Say that again," I said.

"I said they look like they were playing volleyball instead of—"

I grabbed Chuck and danced around. "Chuck, you're a genius. Guys! Listen up. Skinny, instead of trying to catch the ball when it's thrown to you, hit it like a volleyball over to Shorty and let him catch it. That should get us a couple yards."

Uncle Marshall walked to the center of the

field and blew his whistle. "Let's begin the second half!" he yelled.

Jerry's team lined up to receive. "I'm holding the ball for the kickoff," yelled Fats as he placed the ball down on the ground. Doc took a running start and kicked a high, long, spiraling kick. Best kick of the day, I thought. One of Jerry's campers tried to catch it but it squirted out of his hands. Three others tried to pick it up but it slipped away from them, too, and rolled farther down the field. The ball finally came to rest in the end zone at the same time Fats arrived and he promptly fell on it for a score. Jerry—14, Me—7.

"WHAT'S THE MATTER WITH YOU GUYS?" yelled Jerry in disgust.

"The ball was extra slippery," yelled one of his kids back. "It felt like it was covered with gooey, slimy, melted chocolate."

That's because it was covered with gooey, slimy, melted chocolate, I thought. *We'll take it any way we can get it.*

Jerry made Uncle Marshall wipe off the ball and we kicked off again. Now Skinny rushed the passer and Lisa was right. The third quarter ended with no further scoring.

Midway through the last quarter I signaled for my team to use Chuck's volleyball play. Whiney passed the ball to Skinny, but instead of catching it, he tapped the ball to Shorty. Shorty then tapped the ball to Doc, who tapped it to the Brain, who tapped it to the Spaz, who tapped it to Fats, who tapped it back to Whiney, who caught it, and ran in for the touchdown. Jerry—14, Me—14.

Jerry threw his clipboard down on the ground at the same time I threw mine up in the air. "###@@@###@@@@@!" yelled Jerry just loud enough for Uncle Marshall to turn around and give him the evil eye.

"WE'RE NUMBER ONE!" chanted my team as they lined up to kick off to Jerry's team again.

"SCORE ONE MORE!" chanted Jerry's team.

There were only two minutes left in the game. A tie would be a moral victory. Unfortunately Skinny's kick was a short one and Jerry's team started at midfield. Their first three plays went nowhere. With less than a minute to go they lined up in punt formation.

"Watch out for the fake kick," I yelled, but no one seemed to hear me.

I was right. Instead of kicking the ball, the punter threw it with all his might. I watched as the ball sailed toward the corner of the end zone, where one of Jerry's kids stood all alone waiting to catch it. As the ball came down the boy took two steps backward and cradled the ball in his arms.

I expected to see Uncle Marshall raise his hands and yell score but instead he yelled, "He's out of bounds. Ball goes over to Richie's team."

"He was in!" yelled Jerry.

Uncle Marshall put his hands on his hips and stared right into Jerry's eyes. "Play ball," he said.

There was only time for one more play. "Fumbleroosky," I yelled from the sideline. The play worked to perfection. Everyone ran to the right after Whiney, thinking he had the ball. This left the Spaz all alone to scoop up the ball and be on his way down the opposite side of the field. There was no way that anyone on Jerry's team could catch him before he crossed the goal line. I couldn't believe it. We were going to win.

Then, for no reason I could see, five yards from the goal line the ball popped out of the Spaz's hand and flew up into the air. It hit him in the center of his forehead and rolled forward into the end zone. Everyone dived for the ball.

"I GOT IT," yelled one of Jerry's campers named Arnie.

"NO, YOU DON'T," screamed Fats as he belly-flopped for the same spot.

"FATS GOT IT!" shrieked Shorty.

"NO, HE DOESN'T. I HAVE IT," insisted Arnie.

"THAT'S NOT THE BALL! IT'S MY CHOCOLATE BAR!"

Suddenly there was a loud pop followed by the shrill sound of Uncle Marshall's whistle. "Game's over," he hollered. "But don't anyone move. We still don't know who's got the ball!"

15

Uncle Marshall pulled kids from each team off the pile until Arnie and Fats were the only two left on the ground.

"I DEFINITELY HAVE IT," persisted Arnie.

"NO, YOU DON'T. I HAVE IT," contended Fats.

Who was telling the truth? "They both have a piece of the ball," said Uncle Marshall. "It must have exploded from all that weight on top of it."

"Arnie got his piece first," declared Jerry, "so it's a tie."

"NO WAY!" I replied. "Fats had his piece first, so WE WIN!"

We both looked at each other and then at Uncle Marshall for a ruling. "I'm not sure what to do," he said. "I have an official touch-football rule-book back in my cabin. Wait here. I'll be back with the decision in a minute."

That was the longest minute of my life. Fred and Jon came over to talk, but I walked away. I wanted to be alone. Jerry, on the other hand, walked around in a circle repeating, "Arnie had it first. That means it's a tie. I know it's a tie. I know it's—"

Both of us saw Uncle Marshall coming up the hill at the same time and we ran over to meet him. In his left hand was a brown book. He pointed to the middle of a page. "It says here on page forty-two, and I quote, 'If a ball explodes and rips in half and two or more players have pieces of the ball, possession belongs to the person with the biggest piece.'" He held up one piece of the ball for everyone to see. "This is Arnie's piece." And then the other. "This is Stanley's piece—and you can see that . . ." Fats's real name is Stanley. I never knew that.

". . . Stanley's, I mean Fats's piece is approx-

imately six centimeters bigger than Arnie's,"
shrieked the Brain.

"That's correct," said Uncle Marshall.

"WE WON! WE WON!" I yelled in harmony with my team.

"You cheated," said Jerry.

"Not fair," echoed his bunk.

"You picked the referee," I said. "Are you saying that Uncle Marshall cheated you?"

Jerry's face turned bright red. "Uh, well, no. It's just that . . . I mean . . . the last play was an illegal play anyway."

"Illegal?" said Lisa as she made her way up from the back of the crowd. "There's nothing illegal about that play."

Jerry got a smug smile on his face. "How would you know?"

"I gave Richie that play," she replied. "I got it from my brothers, who play football. It was invented by the coach at the University of Oklahoma."

"Why didn't you give my team that play?" said Jerry angrily.

"Because your team didn't need any help," replied Lisa.

Jerry looked over at me and then at Lisa. He

began to laugh out loud. "Especially no help from a girl. Let's get out of here, guys." Jerry left followed by his bunk.

I wanted to run after Jerry and deck him but instead I kicked the ground hard with my foot. "I want my bed made by the time I get back to the bunk, slave," I yelled in his direction.

"Are you coming back to our bunk soon?" asked Whiney. "We're going to have a party to celebrate."

"I'll be there in five minutes," I said as I looked around for Lisa. "Don't start without me."

"We won't," said Doc.

I spotted her walking slowly away. "Lisa," I yelled, "wait for a second." When I caught up with her I could see that she was upset. "Don't pay any attention to Jerry. He's a professional jerk."

"Boy, would I like to . . ." Her cheeks were bright red.

"Get him back!" I said.

Lisa's face lit up. "Yeah! But how?"

"I think you should apologize to him," said Chuck, who had appeared from nowhere.

Lisa and I both looked at him. "That's the dumbest suggestion I ever heard," said Lisa.

"Stick around him longer and you'll hear dumber ones," I replied.

"Wait a second," continued Chuck, not seeming to mind our putdowns, "I don't mean really apologize to him."

"How can you apologize to someone and not apologize to someone at the same time?" asked Lisa.

"I can't wait to hear this answer," I said.

"Easy," said Chuck. "Lisa, I want you to go over to Jerry before dinner tonight and tell him to meet you behind the tennis courts at nine o'clock tonight. When he asks why, say you want to talk to him in private about the football play you gave to Richie. Look very upset. If I know Jerry, he'll think you want to apologize."

"Once he comes, then what?" I asked.

"Make him think you're sorry. Make him think you want to kiss and make up."

"Kiss him?" said Lisa. "I'd sooner kiss a frog with the hope of turning him into a handsome prince than kiss Jerry. Yeech!"

Chuck got a sneaky gleam in his eye. "This is where the good part comes in. When Jerry comes over and puckers up for that kiss, that's when you'll turn him down and walk away. That'll fix him good."

Lisa and I nodded in agreement. Chuck's plan was pretty good after all. "Wouldn't it be better to do it at tonight's dance in front of everybody?" I asked. "That would really embarrass him but good."

Chuck smiled. "I thought of that," he said as he opened his Spider-Man™ briefcase and rummaged noisily through it. "Jerry will suspect something if it's done in front of everyone. However, everyone still might get a chance to hear what happens."

I looked over at Lisa and shrugged my shoulders. She looked as puzzled as I felt. "How can everybody hear what happens if nobody but the four of us are there?"

Chuck continued to look through his briefcase. "That's why we need . . . where is it now? . . . oh, here it is. . . ." He held up what looked like a skinny black magician's wand and showed it to Lisa and me. "This."

"What is it?" we asked.

"It's the other half of this," said Chuck as he reached into his case again and produced a small square silver box. Chuck pushed one of the knobs on the front of the box and a section of the top popped up.

"It's a miniature tape recorder," I exclaimed. "But what's the black thing?"

"It's a supersensitive wireless remote control microphone," explained Chuck.

"Where did you get that?" I asked.

"Did you ever put Koko-Froth powder in your milk?"

I'd tried it once. It made the milk look like greenish mud. "It was the worst."

"I only had to pay ten dollars if I sent the labels in from ten jars with my money."

"Ten jars?"

"Three hundred fifty glasses of Koko-Froth-flavored milk."

"You drank . . . ?"

Chuck nodded.

"I think I'm going to be ill," I said.

"It was worth it and it's just what we need for our final payback to Jerry."

"Amazing," said Lisa. "No one has to be around, because you'll record what happens."

Chuck puffed out his chest. "Yup. And I can

change the words around by splicing the tape to say what we want them to say, if we have to."

"Won't Jerry see the microphone if it's on me?" asked Lisa.

Chuck nodded. A sly smile crept onto his face and he looked over at me. "That's where Richie comes in."

16

If Chuck asked you to crawl out on a shaky tree limb fifteen feet above the ground and hold a supersensitive wireless remote control microphone above Jerry and Lisa, would you do it? You wouldn't even have to think a second to answer that question. Then why am I out on a shaky tree limb, fifteen feet above the ground, holding a supersensitive wireless remote control microphone with one hand and the shaky tree limb with the other? "Are you sure I have to be up here for this to work?" I asked.

Chuck raised his flashlight and nearly blinded me. "If the microphone is put any other place, it won't work as well. You do want the recording to be clear, don't you?"

As I nodded, the branch began to wobble. "This branch is going to break any minute and I'm going to be killed."

"Don't move, then," said Chuck as he turned to Lisa. "You know what to say?"

Lisa nodded.

"Make sure that both of you are directly under this branch when you talk. I'll be hiding in the bushes over there working the recorder."

"He's coming," I called down in a loud whisper. Chuck disappeared into a small clump of bushes ten feet away. Lisa paced nervously beneath me. "Good luck," I whispered. She looked up and smiled.

A minute later Jerry appeared. He had the same smug look on his face he had had during the game. "You wanted to say something to me?" he asked.

"You're so far away," said Lisa. "Come closer."

"I can hear you from here," replied Jerry.

So, I risked my life for nothing, I thought. *That figures.*

"I don't like to talk to anyone I can't look in

the eye," said Lisa. Jerry strutted over and stopped directly under me. *Way to go, Lisa. I knew I could count on you.* I lowered the microphone slowly until it was just above Jerry's head.

"Well," said Jerry, "what do you want to tell me?"

Lisa took a step toward Jerry and to my surprise he took a step backward. *You're not supposed to do that,* I said to myself as I slithered down the branch almost to the end. I took a deep breath and stretched my arm out as far as it would go in order to keep the microphone directly above them. "I wanted to talk to you about the football play I gave to Richie."

Jerry began to fidget with his hands and rock back and forth sideways. "Yeah, what about it?" he snapped.

"Well, I just wanted to say that"—Lisa paused and took another step toward Jerry. Again he backed away—"I just wanted to keep the game close, that's all," she said.

Why did Jerry keep backing away? Was Mr. Macho really Mr. Musho? I moved down to the end of the branch and held my breath as it started to sway up and down.

"Well, you shouldn't have done it." His voice sounded less definite than before.

Lisa raised her arms. "Maybe I shouldn't have," she said in the sexiest voice ever, "but that was yesterday. Now all I want to do is . . ." *Come on, Jerry,* I thought, *try and hug her.*

"Stay rrrrright where you are," said Jerry. He looked like he was quivering. "I'm not very good at this."

"Not good at what?" asked Lisa.

"Thhhhat!" This was too good to be true. I leaned down over the end of the branch, not wanting to miss a word of it. Lisa stood there with her mouth open in silence. Jerry folded and unfolded his arms a couple times before putting his hands into his pockets. He wiped his forehead with his sleeve and bit his upper lip. It was great to see him squirm. "You see, I"—his breathing sounded like he had just run a race— "I've never kissed a girl before, so . . . I mean, I . . . never mind."

I threw both arms up in the air and gave a silent cheer. The branch shook in time to my excitement and I slowly felt myself slipping off. I clutched the branch with both hands, frantically trying to stop my slide. Below me Jerry paced around in a circle. No one said a word.

Suddenly the silence was broken by the sound of something cracking. As I felt the branch give way under me I scrambled to get back to the tree trunk. Before I could say, "Why am I out on a shaky tree limb, fifteen feet above the ground, holding a supersensitive wireless remote control microphone with one hand and the shaky tree limb with the other?" I was plummeting downward.

I felt a sharp pain in my elbow as it hit Jerry's face and the microphone went flying out of my hand. Jerry collapsed in a heap and I ended up on top of him. I don't know how long we were lying there, but when I realized where I was, I struggled to my feet. Neither Lisa nor Chuck was anywhere in sight, so I headed off into the night.

When I got back to the bunk it was empty. My right elbow was badly bruised and bleeding, so I washed it off with cold water and wrapped it in a towel.

An out-of-breath Chuck appeared a minute later, covered with dirt. "Are you all right?" he panted.

I took off the towel and showed him my elbow. "It's a little scraped. Nothing serious. Did you get the recording?"

Chuck took a minute to catch his breath. "Listen for yourself," he said as he pushed the play button.

"I've never kissed a girl before, so . . . I mean, I . . . never mind."

"Chuck, you're a genius."

Chuck puffed out his chest and smiled. "Wanna hear the branch cracking? It sounds amaaaazing!"

"No, thanks," I replied. "Once was enough."

Just then the door to the bunk opened and in walked Jon and Fred. Chuck casually slipped the recorder into his Spider-Man™ duffel. "Why weren't you at the dance?" asked Jon.

"We were sitting outside," said Chuck. "Right, Richie?"

"R-r-right, Chuck," I stammered, "we were sitting outside in the grass."

The door to the bunk opened once again and in walked Jerry. His shirt was ripped at the collar and he tried to cover the shiner over his left eye with his hand.

"Who gave you that?" asked Fred. Chuck

glanced over at me and winked. Jerry walked into the bathroom without answering.

"What's with him?" asked Fred.

"Beats me," I replied as I crawled under the covers. The warm bed felt good and I fell asleep immediately. I was dreaming about a football game when someone shook me. "Huh? What? What time is it?" When I brushed the blurries out of my eyes I saw it was Chuck.

"Shh," he said. "It's three o'clock in the morning. Get dressed. We still have one more thing to do."

"Three o'clock in the morning!" I blurted out. "Are you crazy?"

"Shhh," whispered Chuck. "Trust me and get dressed."

My elbow still hurt from trusting him, but he did get the recording. What did this fiend have in mind? Where was he taking me? Were we going for another midnight shower? Reluctantly I got dressed and followed Chuck. We ended up at the main office.

"Stand guard here," he said. "I'll be right out and when I am, get on your running shoes."

I waited outside in silence. First I heard him click on the PA system. That was followed by a scratching sound, the kind you hear just before a record begins to play. Then Chuck burst through the door. "Follow me," he yelled. We both ran like hell back to the bunk, and just as we jumped into bed and pulled the covers over our heads, we heard the blaring sounds of a marching band over the PA system.

"Turn off the music!" yelled Fred.

"Quiet!" hollered Jon.

"I wanna sleep," I complained as I rubbed my eyes.

"Who's the stupid jerk that did that?" shrieked Chuck.

The music played for about a minute and then stopped as abruptly as it had started.

The next day after breakfast Jerry found a note and a tape on his bed. I pretended to look at a magazine, but I was really repeating the note over in my mind while I watched him read it.

If you don't want everybody in camp to hear a copy of this tape like they heard the music last night, stop acting like a jerk and join the human race.

Jerry put the tape in his tape recorder and disappeared outside. When he returned he looked like he was almost ready to cry. Even though he had been a show-off and a bully for the better part of four weeks, I felt sorry for him then. Not sorry enough to give him the original tape, but sorry that I had to be so mean to him to make a point. The whole blackmail idea bothered me, but if it got Jerry to change, I guess it wasn't such a bad thing to do.

17

"I don't understand it," said Fred. "For the first half of the summer Jerry acts like the biggest jerk in the world and in the past week he changes and becomes one of the guys."

Chuck looked over at me and then back at Fred. "Yeah, I noticed that too. Isn't it amazing how some people change just like that?"

"He's even given up on Lisa," said Jon, looking at me. "Now she's all yours."

Everything was working out just as Chuck and I had planned. I should feel happy, then, right? I had felt happy for a little while, but not anymore. Over the past couple days I'd felt guilty, as if I'd done something wrong. "Things are working out great," I replied in an unconvincing manner. *But I haven't done anything wrong. Have I?* Nothing made very much sense. "What are you doing with your bunk this morning?" I asked, purposely changing the subject.

"Major-league hiking again," complained Fred.

"Nature," replied Jon.

"Arts and crafts," said Chuck. "What about you?"

"My bunk has football," I replied.

"How come your bunk gets all the good activities?" asked Fred.

"Try coaching them at football and see how good it is," I replied on my way out the door. "It's not just a job. It's an adventure!" When I got to the football field it was empty, so I sat down on the bleachers and waited for my bunk to arrive. Sitting by myself only made things worse.

"Why do we have to play football today?" asked Shorty. I looked up. The champs had arrived.

"Yeah," chimed in Skinny. "We won the

championship last week. Isn't that enough football for one summer?''

"I'd rather do some hiking," said Fats. "We
can hike down to the kitchen, pack up a lot of
supplies, and then hike back to our bunk and
have lunch."

"Will you guys stop complaining," I said,
"and line up? I want to try to teach you how to
really catch a ball today."

"According to my calculations, Fats, if you
run as hard as you can for this whole period,
without stopping once, you might burn up half
of one of those eight pieces of French toast you
had for breakfast."

"According to my calculations," replied Fats,
"if I sit on you right now you won't be able to
calculate anything for a long time."

"Oh, yeah?" barked the Brain.

"Yeah!"

"Cut it out, guys," I said. "Spaz, you're up
first. Go out ten steps and turn around. The ball
will be there waiting for you."

The Spaz ran out ten steps and turned. I
floated a soft pass in his direction. The ball hit
him squarely in the chest and ricocheted onto
the next playing field. He started to run over to

get it, but he stopped when he saw Jerry pick up the ball. As Jerry came toward him with the ball, he began backing away. As usual his feet became tangled and he landed on his butt with a thump.

"You'll never catch a ball that way," said Jerry as he helped the Spaz up to his feet. "First of all you took your eyes off the ball. Second, you let it hit you in the chest. Next time Richie throws you a pass . . ."

I watched as Jerry tried to teach the Spaz the basics of catching a football. Would he still be acting like this if I gave him back the tape? Probably not. And even though he was much more likable now, was blackmail the right way to do it? I decided to talk to Chuck about giving the tape back. As soon as the period was over I ran down to the bunk to look for Chuck.

When I got to the porch Chuck's was the first voice I heard. "I don't know what tape you're talking about!" he yelled.

I walked quietly over to the window and looked in. I saw Jerry push Chuck against the wall with both hands. "Don't lie to me," he yelled. Chuck looked petrified. "Give me the tape or I'll break your face."

"Get off of me," said Chuck. "I don't have any tape of yours."

Jerry pushed Chuck backward again. "I'm only going to ask you one more time," he said as he made a fist and waved it in Chuck's face. I started to go in to help, but something inside told me to stay put.

"Okay, okay," said Chuck. "I'll give you the tape." He walked over to his bed and pulled out the Spider-Man™ duffel. He rummaged through it for a minute and returned with the tape cradled in his hand. "Here. You want the tape. It's yours."

Jerry had a slimy smirk on his face as he reached for the tape. Suddenly Chuck pulled his hand back and then just as suddenly let it fly forward. His fist and the tape landed in the center of Jerry's face with a loud crack that sent him reeling backward over a bed and onto the floor. I heard loud moaning before I saw Jerry pull himself up and head for the door. Blood-soaked hands covered his nose.

Chuck's expression was a mixture of surprise and concern. "Are you all right?" he yelled. "I didn't mean to hurt you."

Jerry didn't look back as he bolted from the

bunk. I think he saw me out of the corner of his eye, but he never stopped running until he disappeared into the woods.

Chuck was staring at his fist in amazement and shaking as I came in. Without saying a word I walked over to him and gave him a high five. "Do you think I broke his nose?" he asked.

"If anything is shattered, it's his pride," I replied. "Where is the tape now?"

Chuck opened his hand. The case had splintered, but the tape itself was okay.

"Give it to me."

"That's a good idea," said Chuck. "You keep it."

"I'm giving it back to Jerry," I said.

"You're what?" he replied in disbelief.

"Giving it back," I replied.

"I JUST RISKED MY LIFE to keep Jerry from getting the tape and now you're giving it back. Why?"

"Because."

"I don't understand," said Chuck.

"We didn't like it when Jerry pushed us around and now we're doing exactly the same thing to him."

"It's different," said Chuck.

"It's not different," I replied. "I refuse to act like him anymore." I held out my hand and waited for Chuck to give me the tape. I could tell by the serious expression on his face that he was thinking about what I had said.

Finally Chuck handed me the tape. "Now he'll definitely start acting like he did before."

"He already has," I said as I headed out of the bunk for the woods. It wasn't long before I found Jerry sitting under a tree. His hands were still covering his nose.

"Get out of here," he yelled.

I tossed Jerry the tape. "Here," I said as it landed beside him.

Jerry picked up the tape and tossed it back to me. "Forget it," he said. "I'm leaving."

"Why?" I asked. "There're only two more weeks left."

"Chuck's gonna tell everyone what happened."

"You don't know Chuck very well," I replied as I sat down beside him. "Your first mistake was pushing him the way you did. Everybody has their limit. Even the biggest nerd can only be pushed so far." Here I was sounding like my father again. "Your second mistake is thinking he'll brag about what he did. That's something you would do, but not Chuck. I'm going back to the bunk now."

Jerry stood up and took his hands away from his nose. The bleeding had stopped but it was red and swollen. He extended his bloody hand and we shook. We walked back to the bunk together in silence.

Fred was the first one to see us when we walked in the door. "What happened to you?" he asked.

At first Jerry didn't answer.

"You look like you ran into a brick wall," said Jon. "How did it happen?"

Jerry opened his mouth and started to say something, but Chuck interrupted him. "I did it," he said. His chest was puffed out and he had a triumphant look on his face. "I did it," he said again. "Jerry and I were playing soccer. He was in goal and I was coming in for a shot. He dove for the ball just as I went to kick it."

"Did you score?" asked Fred.

"He scored, all right," said Jerry, looking over at Chuck. "He scored."

153

I was sitting on my bed trying to decide what I was going to wear to the final social at the lake when Chuck appeared. He had a sheepish grin on his face. "What are you doing?" he asked.

"I'm picking out my clothes for tonight," I replied.

"I've been meaning to talk to you about that," said Chuck.

"No way! Forget it! Don't mention it," I roared. "It's out of the question! End of discussion. Final!"

"Wait a minute," said Chuck. "You don't even know what I'm going to say."

I knew exactly what Chuck was going to say and I was having no part of it. "Okay, what do you want?"

"Tonight at the lake social I would like to—"

"Double-date with me tonight. Just like I said before. No way."

"You're not being fair," said Chuck.

"I'm not being fair? Every time I see a boat I start to remember what happened last year. There I was trying to help you stop your nosebleed, and how did you show your thanks? You knocked me out of the boat and barfed all over me."

"I didn't do it on purpose," said Chuck.

"I don't care. There is NO WAY you will be in the same rowboat with me ever again, and that's final." I had started to walk out of the bunk when Chuck grabbed my arm.

"Listen for a second," he pleaded.

I stopped and folded my hands.

"I haven't had a nosebleed or thrown up since this time last year."

I continued to shake my head no.

"You have to let me go with you!"

"I have to what?" I asked.

"You have to let me go," repeated Chuck. "If

it wasn't for me and my help, you'd be going in the rowboat all by yourself."

"How can you be sure Lisa will go with me?" I asked.

"Who else would she go with?" said Chuck.

"Jerry's been acting pretty nice lately. Maybe Lisa will want to go with him."

"Well, if she does go with you, can I double?"

"Okay," I said reluctantly. "But if you look green, if you look nauseous, if you look funny, which you do most of the time, I will personally throw you overboard myself! Is that clear?"

Chuck shook his head up and down and patted me continuously on the shoulder. "Thanks, Richie. You won't regret this. Thanks. Thanks."

For the rest of the afternoon I practiced what I was going to say to Lisa to get her to be my date. I'd start out by asking her if she liked rowing around the lake. I already knew she did because I'd seen her out there rowing around with her girlfriends. Then I'd tell her that my favorite rowboat was the big green one with the yellow stripe on the side and I'd say, "Let's go down and see it." After that I'd have it made.

I didn't consider it going any other way until that night. I had just put on my best pair of jeans and a U2 T-shirt when I thought, *What if she says she doesn't want to see the boat? Then I say . . . what will I say? I just tell her . . .* no, that wouldn't work. When I finally left the bunk and made my way to the lake, my question still remained unanswered.

I spotted Lisa standing with her girlfriends. Still no answer. Twenty-five feet away from Lisa and counting. I forced a smile. No answer yet. We're face-to-face. "Hi." Try to look relaxed. "Great night for rowing around on the lake, isn't it?"

Lisa smiled. "What are we waiting for, then?"

"I was wondering if you liked to . . . you mean you will?" I wanted to leap up into the air and yell, but I didn't. *You were so smooth, Richie,* I thought, *you are the essence of coolness.*

Chuck was already waiting for me on the dock with his date. She was a short red-haired girl named Judy. In her left hand she carried a briefcase with a picture of Wonder Woman on it. A match made in turkey heaven, I thought. "See, I told you she'd go with you," he yelled. I

157

buried my face in my hand just as I heard Chuck
say, "Oops!"

When I finally had the courage to look over
at Lisa, she didn't seem angry. Maybe she hadn't
heard. Nevertheless, if I had a chance to drown
Chuck when we got to the middle of the lake,
I'd do it. The jury would surely understand it
was self-defense. "Did you pick out a boat for us
yet?" I asked.

"The green one with the yellow stripe," he
replied with fear in his eyes. "It's big enough to
fit another couple, so I asked Jerry and his date
to come with us too. Okay?"

Being with Jerry might be better than being
with Chuck, I thought. "Great," I said. "Jerry
should be right behind me."

Lisa pointed to Judy's bag. "What's in there?"

"You'll see," said Judy.

"I have this all planned out," said Chuck just
as Jerry and his date arrived. "To start, Richie
will sit in the front of the boat; Lisa, Judy, and I
will sit in the back; and Jerry and Erica will row.
We'll switch seats every half hour. Okay?"

"I'm the best at rowing," boasted Jerry. "The
week before camp I went rowing for seven
hours without resting one minute."

Chuck and I turned to look at Jerry at the same time. His face immediately got beet-red.

"I mean I went rowing for one hour without . . ."

Chuck and I continued to stare.

"I really rowed for ten minutes."

At least he's trying, I thought. As everybody climbed into the boat I grabbed Chuck by the arm and whispered, "I changed my mind. If you get sick, I'll kill you on the spot and throw your remains to the fishes."

"Don't worry, Richie," said Chuck. "I promise, Scout's honor, I won't get sick. But even if I do, I'm at one end of the boat and you're at the other, so nothing's going to happen to you. See, I've got everything covered."

As I untied the boat, Chuck pulled his briefcase out from under the backseat and took out his tape recorder and some wires. Judy reached into her case, took out two minispeakers, and connected them to Chuck's recorder. Chuck slipped in a tape and pushed play. The melodious sounds of my favorite rock group, the Peanut Butter Elephant, filled the boat. I could feel it. This was going to be the best night of my life. Jerry and Erica rowed until we got to the middle of the lake. I was listening to the music and looking at Lisa when I heard a shrill-pitched buzzer. Chuck pushed something on his watch and stood up. "Time to switch places. Jerry, you go to the front. Erica, you go to the back. Richie, you come back here with Lisa, and Judy and I will row. Okay, everybody switch now!"

The boat began to rock as everyone started to change places. I didn't think very much about it until Judy said in an almost inaudible voice, "This rocking is making me sick." *Chuck probably put her up to this,* I thought as I inched my way toward the middle of the boat. "I feel very sick," repeated Judy. This time her voice was louder and she was serious.

"Go back to the end of the boat," yelled Chuck. Judy panicked, and in her confusion she charged toward me in the front. "The other end of the boat," yelled Chuck, "the other end," but Judy didn't listen. Her hand was over her mouth and she looked green.

I had to think fast. I ran to the front of the boat and stood up on the seat. If I jumped in now I'd be a safe enough distance away from the boat by the time she got there. It was the only sensible thing to do. Judy yelled something just as I pushed off the seat and arced my dive outward. The water was much colder and muddier than I remembered. I stayed underwater until I was sure I was far enough away from the boat, and then I came up for air.

I wiped the water away from my eyes and tried to focus on the boat. "Richie! Richie! Are you all right?"

"I'm fine," I said as I swam toward the boat. "How's Judy?"

"I'm fine," she said. "That was the strangest feeling I ever had—one minute I felt like I had to throw up, and the next minute I feel fine. Like nothing happened. I yelled for you not to jump, but you were already in the air."

Figures, I thought grimly. *Just you wait.* I raised my hands up to be pulled in. Chuck and Judy grabbed my right arm while Jerry and Erica grabbed my left. Instead of pushing off from the pond bottom and helping them, I planted my feet in the muck and yanked. The four of them tumbled over the side into the water. I scrambled into the boat and grabbed the oars. As I rowed away I yelled to Fred, who was rowing over behind them. "I think they need a lift."

"We'll get you later," they screamed in unison, but I kept on rowing. I was alone at last with Lisa.

"That wasn't very nice," she said as she sat down next to me, "but it was pretty funny."

I looked at Lisa sitting there next to me and everything bad that had happened to me this summer faded. The moon was full, just like in the songs. I put my arm around her and moved closer. I wasn't sure I knew how to kiss right, but something inside told me this was the time. As I leaned over and puckered my lips, I saw Lisa close her eyes. I closed mine, too, but quickly opened them ever so slightly just to make sure I wouldn't end up kissing her nose. Her cold lips made me feel warm all over. I smiled and I could tell she did too.

I guess the next thing I expected to hear was music, since that's the way it is in the movies, but instead I heard water splashing and then giggling. When I opened my eyes I saw seven giggling gawking geeks rowing toward us.

"Wanna chocolate bar?" asked Fats.

"FIGURES!!"

19

Dear Richie,

By the time you get this letter camp will be almost over.

Another boring letter from my mother, I thought, and I folded it up and put it into my back pocket. Why I took it out again to finish I'll never know.

I know we promised to pick you and Chuck up at the end of camp, but Dad was called away unexpectedly on business and my car is in the shop with transmission trouble. So I called Chuck's family and they said it would be no problem to pick you and Chuck up and bring you home.

"NO PROBLEM!" I yelled. "NO PROBLEM? Sure. It's not a problem for you. You don't have to be hummed at for two hours, rocked back and forth until you're seasick, and treated like a fire hydrant by an overaffectionate Labrador. I'm not going. I'd sooner walk."

"Hiiiii, Richie."

Without looking up I knew it was Lisa. "Hi, Lees," I muttered.

"You don't sound very happy," she replied.

"I'm not. I just got a letter from my mom telling me she can't pick me up and take me home after camp. I have to go home with Chuck's parents."

"So?" she asked. "What's wrong with that?"

"What's wrong with it? On the way up . . . I don't even want to go into it. Take my word for it. The ride up with his family was a disaster. I'm going to walk home. That's all there is to it."

"How 'bout if I ask my parents if you can come with us?" said Lisa.

"If I leave camp at nine in the morning I should be able to get home by . . . Go home with you? Me?"

Lisa nodded.

"Sure. Great," I said. "Go call your parents now to see if it's okay."

All the boy and girl CITs waited up on the baseball field for their parents to pick them up. One by one they were picked up, until the only three left were Lisa, Chuck, and I.

"It wasn't that I didn't want to ride home with you," I said, "it was just that Lisa asked me to go with her, and you wouldn't want me to turn her down, would you?"

"No sweat," said Chuck. "I'd sooner ride home with a girl than with you, any day."

"Mmmmm^{mmmmmmmm}mmmmm^{mmmmmmmmm}mmm mm^{mmmmmmm}mmmmmmmm."

"My parents are here," said Chuck.

Woof woof. Bark bark. Woof woof. Bark bark.

"Great. They brought Oliver and Godzilla."

"Godzilla?" I said.

"Oliver's brother," said Chuck.

I helped Chuck put his baggage in the car and said good-bye. I breathed a sigh of relief. For once I had made the right choice.

I could picture exactly how it would be. Lisa would sit next to me in the backseat of the car. For two hours we'd talk and joke around and it would be amazing. I'd want to put my arm around her but I couldn't with her mom in the front, so I'd inch over and squeeze her hand. Lisa would squeeze my hand back and smile.

"That's our station wagon," said Lisa as a red wagon pulled onto the field.

We wouldn't have to talk the whole time. Just being almost alone with her would be great.

"Oh, what a wonderful surprise," continued Lisa. "My mom came with my aunt and Ricky, Tommy, and Donny."

"Ricky, Tommy, and Donny?" I said.

"My one-year-old cousins. They're triplets and are they cute."

"Triplets? One-year-old triplets??? OLLLLL-LIVER! GODZILLAAAAAA! CHUCK-IEEEEEEE!!! WAIT FOR MEEEEEEE!!!!!"